It's the Characters!

ISABEL PABÁN FREED

For my friends

An uninstructed mass, feeling its way to revolution, usually
begins by terrorism.
— C. L. R. James

One

— Who assassinates a novelist?

— Assassinates?

— It seemed like an assassinate.

— …

— …

— You've been fucked up about this.

— It's not normal for someone you know to be assassinated.

— Now you worry about normal.

— I thought she was alright.

— …

— Friendly, had a cool girlfriend.

— You don't think it was the girlfriend then?

— I am actually asking you to be rabbinical.

— It's Shabbat.

— So?

— It's my day off.

— That can't be how it works.

— …

— …

— This is dead by the way.

— That's tragic.

— And seeing as it is Shabbat-

— I rolled two.

— That was two.

— …

I roll a third spliff.

— If you'd be so kind.

I light it.

— Thank you.

— . . .

— So.

— . . .

— You're fucked up because your client was murdered-

— Assassinated.

— And as her dealer, you feel somehow responsible.

— Courier, and what are you talking about?

— Just shooting the shit.

— I don't think we should smoke a fourth one.

— This one's canoeing.

— She was shot in her own home. No evidence. No witnesses. Police are clueless. It's suspicious.

— I don't think it's your job to be suspicious.

— Isn't it the right thing to be?

— What difference would it make if it was?

— . . .

— . . .

— I thought you weren't working. Go back to being an asshole.

— I am being an asshole.

— . . .

— . . .

He ashes.

— What'd you say this strain was called again?

— This is Seafoam Green.

— What did we have last time?

— Red.

— I liked Red.

— Yeah, Red was good.

— . . .

— . . .

— . . .

He's zoning out.

— You seem nicely cooked.

— I am.

— You have all your food and everything?

— I do.

— Then I'm gonna bounce.

— Sounds good.

— I will see you next week.

— Yes.

— Unless you find some time in your busy schedule.

— You should try not to think too much about the assassination.

— . . .

— This kind of thing happens.

— Does it?

— Didn't it?

I open the door and step out of his apartment.

Waiting for the Bus Home

It's wet but not raining. A group of coworkers is drunk outside the cookie shop. One's loud.

A woman is sleeping at the bus stop.

Some couples walk past, mostly men.

Someone else is waiting for the bus. They're looking across the street and frowning. Another yeller. He's homeless. A woman walks past, staring into the ground. The owner of one of the pizza places stands in the doorway and projects authority; his is open, but the restaurant two down is closed for the night. Maybe a seafood place now. A bus going the other way rolls into the stop, stops, and sinks. The side says, *What if you only needed one app?* There's a logo that looks like every other logo. He gives up when the bus leaves.

— You got the time hon?

— . . . 10:33.

— Bless you.

The other person waiting for the bus is looking at me. Now they're not.

But there's the bus, coming out of the fog at the top of the hill, like it hasn't noticed.

On the Bus Home

Shot in the forehead. No signs of struggle. Girlfriend says she was out of the house. Roommate says he was out of the house. Neighbors weren't home. No signs of forced entry. Known depressive, but suicide has been ruled out, on account of the ballistics. Police are unable to comment further. The investigation is still ongoing. Who assassinates-

An Incident on the Bus Home

The slapped-out headphone bounces near my feet. The slapper says nothing; the slapped is speechless. The driver yells.

The bus stops. The slapper gets off; the slapped picks up the headphone—teens.

One more stop.

Bathroom Surprise

There's a wetsuit hanging in the shower.

Two

— There was another one this week. In Austin. Strangled to death.

— This is serious.

— I've been saying.

— I've never seen canoeing this bad. Isn't this your job?

— This is yours!

— You are not, as far as I am aware, a member of my congregation.

— I'm a Jew in crisis.

— . . .

— Also your friend.

— You think this is crisis?

It is canoeing.

— You need a hobby.

— . . .

— And maybe a real job.

— I have a real job.

— You have an excuse to see people with real jobs.

— It pays fine.

— . . .

— Better than you think.

— ...

— I don't want kids.

— Only roommates?

— This is dead.

— So it is. Would you like to hear an instructive parable?

— Not really.

— ...

— Is there something you need to workshop?

— I'm chilling.

— ...

— ...

— ...

— My parents asked about you, by the way.

— Oh, tell them I said hi. How are they?

— They're good.

— That's good.

— ...

— Should we watch something?

About Seven Minutes of *One Stone* (2022)

An establishing shot of a nice-looking island is overlaid with the words *Somewhere in the Pacific*; it quickly becomes the inside of a lab, or somewhere else science happens, although, in this case, science appears not to be happening, as the two scientists throw crumpled-up pieces of paper into a wire basket, miss, and make a series of quips—one of the scientists has a familiar face and is considerably more serious-seeming than the other, who, it's safe to assume, is the comic relief; this is his breakout role, and they both have bad hair. Neither are women, but this third scientist is, and she looks at them disdainfully, as if to say, boys. The boys swivel to face a monitor that is now beeping. More quips. The beeping stops, and a series of expository questions reveal that the more serious-seeming scientist has a daughter back home, whom he misses, and a passion for geothermal energy, which is the future of our planet, and also why he's here today, on this island somewhere in the Pacific. There is now a reinvigorated beeping. The serious woman scientist and the serious man scientist confer as to this potentially serious situation, speculating that the island's chief volcano may be erupting—*it's not the volcano*, says the comic relief, as he stands by the window, seriously. An otherworldly squawk. Title sequence.

 — That's unfortunate.

 — What?

 — I was hoping they'd show it.

 — They never show it.

 — Yeah, but give us a talon or something.

 — A talon would've been nice.

Back at the Bus Stop

A pigeon hops out of the way. Others join it.

The neon sign above the tourist trap may as well be flickering.

New Client

— Like a CSA, exactly.
— But weed?
— But weed.

Unusually High on the Job

Sun's out.
— Can I help you?
— I've got a delivery from Solidarity Greens.
— Didn't order shit.
— 1237?
— That's the other bell.
— My bad.
Didn't have to slam it.
Sun's really out.
— You must be with Solidarity Greens! I saw you from the window. Did you hit the wrong bell?
— Ah, yeah.
— Sorry about that!
— It's no worries.
— Well, come in, come in.
Nice apartment.
— Shoes off?
— If you don't mind, thank you.
— No problem.
— ...
— ...

— So, I have to admit, I am not very experienced with all this. I tried it once in college, but since then . . . it's just . . . I haven't really been wanting to write.

— I've heard it's good for that.

— And so there I was, talking to one of my other writer friends, and she had mentioned this service she was . . . she . . .

She looks so sad.

But now she's laughing.

— I'm sorry. I'm sure it's not easy for you either.

— Sorry?

— She was always going on and on, I just assumed.

— Oh, I-

Laughing again,

— What am I saying? She was like that.

What.

— There's a memorial service tomorrow, at 5. You should come.

— Where is it?

— One of her friend's apartments. I have the address on my phone . . . here.

— Thanks.

— . . .

— . . .

— I remember being scared.

— Sorry?

— The last time I smoked. In college. Everything was so scary. We tried to watch TV. Some stupid sitcom. I spent the night in a ball on my friend's floor.

— That can happen.

— What should I do if it does?

— Try to remember that everything's supposed to feel different.

— I see.

Oven's on.

— Sunchokes. The season's about to end.

— Don't think I've ever had a sunchoke.

— . . .

— . . . well, here is your weed. There's a few different strains in there, and a little sheet explaining them. Since this is your first time in a while, I'd recommend starting with the Chartreuse. It's a little more whimsical. Also, since this is your first order with us, we threw in some edibles, also from local farms. These can take a while to hit, so good to be patient.

— Thank you.

— No problem. Thank you for inviting me in. This is a lovely apartment.

— Oh, you think so? My husband did most of it . . . I'll see you tomorrow, then?

— For sure, I'll try to drop by.

— Take care . . .

It's still nice out. Everyone's walking their dogs.

Another J, Plus the Store

I'm among the legumes. Beans. Beans. Beans. Lentils. Beans. Lentils. Beans. What is he staring at?

The Memorial Service

— Like a CSA, exactly.

— Cool.

— You said you worked together?

— Met in college. Same freshman dorm. We were friends all four years, then I stayed for a master's and she moved up here . . . she actually referred me for the job I have now, so we ended up being coworkers too. Different teams, though. And when the pandemic hit we went remote, so I only saw her outside of work after that.

— Gotcha.

— Have you been at your job long?

— I think this is my fourth year.

— So almost straight out of college then.

— I didn't finish-

Someone is touching my shoulder.

— You're here. Wonderful. I'm so glad you could make it.

What is her name?

— Oh, hey. Yeah, thought I'd stop by for a bit.

— Well, I'm very glad you did. I just had a lovely conversation with your friend over there.

Ah, he's here.

Now this guy's touching my shoulder.

— Listen, I have to head out, but it was nice meeting you. Solidarity Greens, right?

— Right, exactly. Nice meeting you too.

He leaves.

[12]

— I'm afraid I also have . . . someone I should talk to.

— Alright.

She leaves.

There's too many people for this apartment. But I'll go to him.

— So, you do have some time in your busy schedule.

— This is my busy schedule. Her family asked me to stop by.

— Gotcha.

— . . .

— It's a nice place.

— It is a nice place.

— . . .

— . . .

Something's happening one circle over.

— Please don't . . . sorry, just . . . no one tells you what you're supposed to do when your girlfriend gets shot in your fucking apartment.

— You're-

— Doing the best I can?

— . . .   — . . .   — . . .   — . . .

— I'm not, okay? I'm-

— Broken.

There he goes.

— What.

— You're broken.

— . . .

— This farmer has a problem: the great bird Ziz keeps destroying his house. The farmer rebuilds the house. The great

bird Ziz destroys it. The farmer rebuilds the house. The great bird Ziz destroys it. One day, after the house has once again been destroyed, the town's junior rabbi visits the farmer. *Why do you rebuild your house each time, if you know the great bird Ziz is going to destroy it?* he asks. The farmer looks at the town's junior rabbi. *Rabbi*, he says, *I need a house.*

— …

— When you build your life around someone, and they disappear, you break.

— …

— …   — …   — …   — …   — …

— So I …

— Yes.

— … thank you.

She looks grateful. They look relieved.

He turns back and walks toward me.

— Nice.

— Yes. I take my work seriously.

— …

— Something you might consider.

— That was implied.

— …

— Don't look at me like that.

— This is serious.

Now she's looking at me.

— I know …

Really looking.

— … I know.

— …

— I think I may need to leave.

On the Street

The woman in front of me's on the phone speaking Spanglish and gesturing with her hands; she doesn't cede the right of way and, as she crosses, looks the other direction down an empty street. There's a bleach stain on the back of her hoodie.

I turn right and pass the school. Nobody's on the steps; there's an abandoned trash cart out front.

The J clanks by.

It's getting dark.

They've fenced off the flat part of the park. A couple sits on a blanket a bit up the hill, drinking tallboys. One laughs, like she wasn't expecting to. The other looks proud of herself, then, when this is commented on, somewhat sheepish. This is also commented on. She pretends to hide behind her beer.

Another phone call walks by.

Another.

Scattered blankets on the other side. Couples, friend groups—that guy's by himself, still reading.

Just missed the crosswalk. Some skateboarders are bombing down the hill. Someone honks.

A sidewalk sale is wrapping up.

He's walked her down to say goodbye, but neither wants to say goodbye; the driver has their hazards on.

Someone's taking out the trash.

Paying at the Taqueria

The wife this time. She smiles.

Doubling Back

Sidewalk sale is still wrapping up.
Couple's gone.
The J again.

Home, Obliterated on the Better Couch

— Okay it was crazy like I'm there, waiting for the bus, and I'm sweaty, like so sweaty, and I see this person staring at me, and all I can think about is how sweaty I am, but then they ask me for the time, so I pull out my phone and tell them, but I think they just wanted to hear my voice because the next thing they say is, *So I couldn't help but notice you were trans, and I'm actually recently trans myself, although I don't really know which way I'm going, and I just wanted to ask, like, what has your experience been?*

— *What has your experience been?*

— Yeah!

— Wild.

— I know!

— What'd you say?

— I was like, yeah it's been okay, ups and downs. And then we get on the bus and they start asking me all these random questions like if I play music, and I'm like, no, and they're like, *You should really play music.*

— Wild.

— They bartend around the corner, actually.

Obliterated at the Bar around the Corner

— Oh.

She looks disappointed.

— They're not here.

— Bummer.

Asleep

Zzz.

Three, Four, and Five

— You good?

— Three novelists dead in a car crash in upstate-

— I heard you, which is why I'm asking: are you good?

— …

— …

— She was staring at me.

— Who was?

— The girlfriend. At that memorial service. And when I was delivering to the person who invited me, she was saying some weird shit about how she thought we were close.

— Were you?

— I just brought her weed!

— …

— I'm going to roll another.

— I wouldn't.

— …

— She's grieving.

— ...

— They both are. You shouldn't place so much weight on a look.

— ...

— Besides, people like to look at you.

— ...

— You're distinctive-looking.

— So relieved to be *distinctive-looking*.

— Happy to help.

— ...

— Do you want to know what I think?

— ...

— ...

— Sure.

— Your life is basically empty-

— Please don't start with this.

— You're right. Your life is perfect.

— It's not perfect; it's fine. My life is fine. I don't need it to be anything more than fine.

— Has it occurred to you that maybe other people need your life to be more than fine?

— Literally who.

— ...

— I get shot in the forehead tomorrow, and-

— Yeah, finish that thought.

— ...

— No, go on.

— ...

— ...

— …
— …
— …
— …
— …
— …
— …
— Sorry.

A Good Several Later

— Because who is like yes, let's close out this album by turning into a donkey?
— A genius.
— A fucking genius.

Fucked Up in the 24-Hour Diner

Some people my age are sitting in the window booth. They're all coming down from acid, except for the trans one, who just got off the bus—she happened to be up. Three of them order pancakes; she orders a breakfast sandwich and a coffee. They're talking about something that happened when they were in college. As she listens, she puts her head on the other woman's shoulder and smiles.

One of the other booths is full of people on their way to work. The waitress pulls up a chair to take their orders and complains when they leave.

Bus Stop Pole Flier

CHARACTER Study: interested in being part of community research about substance use? Call the number below to see if you are eligible, Monday – Friday, 8 AM to 3 PM.

Saturday Morning Coffee

It's early. The guy's the only one behind the counter.

— Gooood morning. How are you today?

— I'm alright, how're you?

— Gooood, thank you for asking. What can I get you today?

— Can I just get a large black coffee?

— And will that be cash or card?

— I think I have some cash.

— Three dollars please.

— . . .

— For here this time?

The good table is open.

— Yeah.

He goes to get one of the mugs.

— Here you are.

— Thank you.

It's too early for brunch. The woman behind me in line orders two iced coffees, one with cream and sugar, one black. She's wearing sweatpants and a hoodie. The guy knows her but needs to be reminded of her name. He asks about her partner. The woman smiles and says she's still waking up. She sips the black one when it's ready.

Another couple walks in. He's about a foot taller than she is. They scan the menu for a bit, then walk to the counter, passing the old couple on their phones.

A man walks in through the front door; he looks right at me. Isn't-

— Hey, Solidarity Greens, right?

— Right, we met at the uh-

— Memorial service, yeah. How've you been?

— I've been alright, yeah, what about you?

— Good, good.

— . . .

— Listen, kind of a strange question, but it didn't really feel right to ask there.

— Sure.

— Have you ever done any figure modeling?

— . . .

— I have this painting class I'm a TA for, and we've been looking. It'd be once a week, on Thursday nights. A few hours tops.

— I-

— And it's good money.

— Yeah, sure. Here, let me give you my number.

— Great, you can just . . .

His phone's set to black and white.

— . . .

— . . . thanks. Sweet.

— . . .

— Well, I'm going to go order, but I'll text you.

— Alright.

He orders a crepe and a cappuccino and goes to sit outside.

Coffee's strong.

Edible's hitting now.

Day Off

Someone left a Christmas ornament on top of the trash can; it's an elf sitting on a sleigh. I turn right, and there's a blind woman on the ground, screaming for help.

— Help me!

— Hold on, let me-

— Somebody help me!

— Here.

She's up. Doesn't thank me and keeps walking, sweeping her cane. Someone on the other side of the street is staring. They turn away when I see them. The blind woman makes it to the end of the street and turns left. A car drives past, playing cumbia.

It's a busy day at the park. The sun is out. People are on blankets. People are chatting. There's reading; there's smoking; there's dogs; there's jugglers. Spike ball. Someone hauls a cart with a speaker in it, blasting early 2000s jams, and a few ex-frat boys brought tables to play drinking games, though one of them is being used in some sort of DJ situation—did they bring a generator? A lot of half-assed dancing.

— I've got mushrooms, prerolls, edibles.

— I'm alright, thanks.

Two guys wearing frisbee gloves toss a frisbee back and forth.

Daylight Savings

Always forget how different this is.

Phone Call

— Hey, I'm calling about the CHARACTER study . . . right, yeah, saw one of the fliers . . . right . . . yeah . . . about fifteen years . . . okay . . . no, that sounds good, as long as it's not Thursday night . . . alright then . . . yeah, next week . . . I'll see you then.

Text Message

np next thursday sounds good to me

Shabbat

— Shallst we?
— You mean should I?
— . . .
— You can't roll spliffs but you can watch TV?
— Hashem works in mysterious ways.
— . . .
— So, were there more?
— I'm working on it.
— Murders, I mean. Assassinations.
— Oh.
— . . .
— Haven't seen any.
— That's good.

— …

— An upsetting coincidence.

— I guess.

— …

— Did I tell you I'm going to do some modeling? For a painting class.

— How are you feeling about that?

— They'll see what they see.

— That's true.

— And it's good money.

— …

— What's that mean?

— I didn't say anything.

— I can literally hear you thinking it.

— …

— We can't all be junior rabbis.

— I said nothing.

— …

— …

— …

— It's been eight years.

— Hopefully it'll be a lot more.

— …

— …

— You don't get bored?

— There are worse things to be than bored.

— Such as?

— Dead.

— …

— Sorry.

— You're good.

— . . .

— But it's been eight years.

— So?

— So there's more to life than not killing yourself.

— That is easy to say if you've never tried to kill yourself.

— That's why I'm saying it.

— . . .

— You could-

— You're not going to let this go?

— It's your life.

— It's my life.

— . . .

— . . .

— Just think about it.

CHARACTER Study, First Visit

The building is uninteresting. Inside, there's a waiting room, and a hallway, and then another room, where they tell me to wait. Someone knocks at the door.

— Come in.

— Hello, how are you?

— I'm alright, how are you?

— I'm good, thank you for asking. So . . . you're here about the CHARACTER study.

— That's right.

— Good. If you'll read this and sign at the bottom.

Looks pretty standard.

— Thank you. I'll be back in a moment.

She leaves. The room is empty except for a counter and some cabinets. No new messages.

Knocks.

— Come in.

— Thank you.

She's carrying a small wooden box and a stack of magazines. She sets the magazines on the counter and holds the box.

— So this drug-

— Substance.

— Sorry?

— It's not a drug. It's a substance.

— Oh. So this substance . . . what should I expect?

— I'm afraid telling you that may compromise the validity of the study.

— . . .

— . . .

— Can I know how long it's supposed to last?

— It's supposed to last for as long as you hold it, give or take some residual effects.

— Hold it?

She opens the box. Inside is what looks like an obsidian sphere.

— That's it?

— That's CHARACTER.

— So I'll-

— I will leave the room, and you will hold CHARAC-
TER for as long as you want. When you have stopped holding
CHARACTER, I will re-enter the room and ask you some
questions.

— How will you know when I've stopped holding it?

— We'll know.

— . . .

— Good luck.

She leaves the box on the counter and exits the room.

It's heavier than it looks.

I sit in the chair and look around. It's an empty room. Just
the magazines. I get up from the chair and grab one. The cover
is the inside of a fast food place, which is fluorescently lit and
vaguely unclean. There are a few high tables no one is sitting
at; at the counter, a card reader sits in front of a large plastic
shield, behind which a masked teenager stands; two other un-
masked teenagers stand to her left. They appear to be talking
with each other, in the middle of some joke maybe, though
the girl at the register looks so bored, it's as if she can't hear
it. She's backed by a few bright screens that display the menu:
chicken sandwich, spicy chicken sandwich, 4 piece chicken
combo, 6 piece chicken combo, 8 piece chicken combo, bis-
cuits, mac & cheese, coleslaw, sodas; it smells like fried chicken.
Behind me, the door opens, and a woman walks in, passing
me on her way to the counter, where one piece of her un-
clasped bodysuit hangs out the back of her jacket, like a tail;
she hasn't noticed; she's lost in the menu—one of the jok-
ing teens calls out the number 103 and stares at me; I look
down at my left hand, which holds a receipt: 103. I go to the

counter, grab the bag, look inside, and eat one of the fries; it tastes fine; I eat another and then turn around; there's more empty chairs; the only group of people here is laughing at the woman, who is still looking up at the menu, oblivious. One of them looks right at me.

I let go, and CHARACTER dents the floor.

There's a knock at the door.

— Come in.

She looks at the floor, smiles, and then looks at the cover of the magazine.

— Interesting. Did you get anything?

I look in the bag.

— Ash?

The bag disintegrates in my hands.

— Did you see that?

She smiles again and hands me some cash.

— You'll come back next week.

Residual Effects on the Bus

There's a crab leg groping its way out of the cover of that person's book. It retracts as soon as I look at it.

That's her book, isn't it?

Lying in Bed

What the fuck?

Morning Walk

No headphones this time: the main noise is the cars driving past. One of the self-driving ones is stuck at the intersection, or maybe it just saw me walking up; the thing on the top spins and spins. People are walking small dogs. People are walking mid-sized dogs. A woman walks a man out of her house, and they don't seem to know if they should kiss goodbye, so they don't. It's around the time the school opens: I'm behind a kid with a superhero backpack explaining to his mom that he doesn't like eating the lunches she packs; she says that that's not a nice thing to say and that he has to eat the lunch; he punches her on the arm; she yells at him.

The guys are opening up one of the corner stores; there's a blanket outside, but no one is sleeping under it, just an empty yogurt container to its side.

The two morning smokers are at the bus stop. The car with the *SOITBE* license plate is parked further up than usual.

Don't step in that.

Helicopter somewhere.

I turn around near the hospital, where there's a guy in blue scrubs smoking a cig with his mask down. He's holding his phone but not looking at it.

On the way back, there's a food delivery sitting on one of the stoops; the receipt is long, but the bag is small—substitutions, I guess.

Weather Report

It's nice again.

First Time Modeling

The studio's sort of downtown. I hit the buzzer and wait. There are security guards standing up the street. One of them looks at me.

Someone buzzes me in.

There isn't really a lobby, just a hallway. I walk until I see him.

— Hey, glad you made it. How've you been?

— I've been alright, you?

— Good, good. Through here.

Behind all the students are a bunch of windows, looking onto the street.

— One-way glass.

— Gotcha.

I undress behind a screen and walk out. He poses me.

— Like that . . . perfect.

An hour in, someone who looks like me walks by the window. Other people pass. Cars pass. A few bikes. A tech bus. A woman. Another. A man. Another. Another bus. More cars. A scooter.

Friday Morning Texts

hey sorry feeling kind of fucked up today
don't think i'll make it tonight

Immediate Response

No problem, feel better.

House Party Plus One

— Wow, yes, interesting. Whenever I try to explain what I do it's like . . . Senior Product Specialist, not illuminating.

— For sure.

— Oh! There's my ex. I should say hi. Excuse me.

The couches are white and leather. The rug is white and expensive. The art is expensive and bad. The kitchen is full of people. The outside area is full of people. The other outside area is full of people. Both bathrooms have a line. This living room is kind of empty.

— There you are, thought you went home.

— I kind of want to.

— Me too. I think I am twinked out.

— . . .

She looks around.

— Let's go then, yeah?

At a New Bus Stop

— Are you okay?

— Sober, even.

— No like . . . generally.

— . . .

— In life.

— Yeah.

— Just like ever since that like murder or whatever.

— I'm fine.

— Bitch when has anyone who's fine ever said *I'm fine*?

— Just now.

— . . .

— My brain gets like this. It'll pass.

— If you say so.

— . . .

— How long until the bus is here?

17 minutes.

— 17 minutes.

— Fuck me.

— . . .

She pulls a J out of her purse.

— Thoughts?

On the New Bus

It's supposed to feel different.

The New Bus Turns onto a Narrow Street

We hit something as we turn, scrape against it. The driver stops the bus and gets out to look at the damage.

People at the front of the bus are laughing.

She leans over.

— I think it's one of the self-driving cars.

— Wow.

Everyone seems happy. People are talking to their busmates. But this bus isn't going to move.

— Should we get off?
— Yeah.
— …
— …
— Fuck.
— …
— There's another stop up the hill.
— Hmm.
— …
— That does not sound fat bitch accessible.
— I think we can do it.
We climb the hill in silence.
About 50 feet from the stop we hear, then see, the bus.
— Fuck.

Almost Deserted Bus Stop

The only other sign of life is the teenager in a backwards flat brim hat and pajama pants practicing his wheelies in the wrong lane.
The fog rolls in.

Back Home

— I'm pretty dead.
— Same.

Sunday Morning Coworker Call

— Hey, what's up? . . . right . . . sure . . . yeah, no problem, I can cover you . . . by 3? . . . sure, yeah, you can drop the car off whenever . . . okay . . . okay . . . yeah, no problem . . . congratulations, by the way . . . yeah . . . of course, of course.

The Billboards Headed Down 101

Tech bullshit. Tech bullshit. Zionist bullshit. Tech bullshit. Tech bullshit. Tech bullshit. Shen Yun. Tech bullshit. Tech bullshit. Sports. More tech bullshit. More sports. More tech bullshit: AI, AI, AI, AI, AI, HR software, AI. Sports. AI. College. Sports.

A Nice House in the Suburbs

Knock, knock.

Fuck.

— Hi, I'm from Solidarity Greens.

— Hello . . .

— Here is this week's delivery. As usual, there's a few different strains in there, and a little sheet explaining them. This week's special is Mauve. If you've tried Crimson or Cobalt, it's a cross between those. Very relaxing.

— Thank you.

— Well, I'll-

— You look familiar.

— One of those faces.

— Right.

— . . .

— Give me a second, I have some cash.

A sculpture. Wall of books. Pool.

— Here.

Generous.

— Thank you.

— I'll . . .

— Sure. It was good to see you.

— You too.

Fuck.

Sunday Dinner

Red lentils. Garlic. Onion. Spices. Too much salt. Left-over rice.

Second CHARACTER Study

She knocks.

— Come in.

— Ah, it's you.

— . . .

— Well, you know the drill. I leave. You hold.

— Sounds good.

She leaves.

There's a screen this time, mounted on one of the walls. The anime unpauses, and I'm there, on the street, watching a building explode outwards—one large robot is tackling another large robot through its wall. Some debris whizzes by. I hide behind the bus stop. The robots stand up, and the red one uses the thrusters on its feet to fly back about 20 feet; it pulls out a large robotic sword. The gray one stands confidently in the sun; the gray is matte. The red robot approaches, swings the sword, and misses; the gray one wraps its arms around the red one's torso and suplexes it into another office building. It's so loud.

Someone grabs my arm.

— C'mon! We have to get out of here!

I place CHARACTER on the ground. I'm back in the room.

— Can you do one more?

I look for the intercom.

— Okay.

A grocery store this time. There's a woman bent over by the milks. She's not moving. There's something wet by her feet. Blood. Pus?

She turns. Her face is covered in blood and pus. There are strings of flesh, which vibrate when she coughs; some of her teeth fall out.

She snarls. I-

FUCK. That ringing. There's someone else here, holding the shotgun.

— Are you okay?

— WHAT?

— Are you okay?

— . . .

— . . .

— I'm fine.

— . . .

— That was loud.
— You get used to it.
A young boy appears out from behind his legs.
— Another kill, Papa?
He looks me over and shakes his head.
— Looks clean.
— ...
— What's that in your hand?
There's a screech somewhere else in the store. He looks up.
— You stay here.
He goes to the cheese island. A shot. One more.
The boy looks at me, then runs after his dad. Another screech. Another shot.
From the entrance, I hear more people.
— In here!
I let go. I'm back in the room. The ringing's quieter now but still hasn't stopped.
She knocks.
— ...
She knocks again.
— May I come in?
— Yeah.
She comes in.
— Thank you.
— ...
— How was that?
— What do you mean *how was that*?
— How was it?

— What would've happened if I got hurt?

— When?

— When I was . . . in there.

— In where?

— . . .

— Nevertheless, your feedback has been noted. There's a little extra here.

— . . .

— For your troubles.

The Walk Home

I'm walking at exactly the same pace as the woman in front of me, who's on the phone, telling a story about Fleet Week. The woman and her friends are at a bar, and they're already kind of drunk when four marines walk in. The marines don't ask to sit with them—they just do it. The leader says something about being on a mission to win the hearts and minds of the civilian population. *We've lost wars before*, he says, *because we did not win the hearts and minds of the civilian population.* He tells her friend that he's in charge of one hundred marines. Her friend swirls the straw in her gin and tonic and asks if that's hard. One of the other marines, who hasn't been listening, butts in to say that the leader is in charge of one thousand marines. They explain things about their uniforms and ask the women what they do. After a bit, the woman and her friends suggest they meet up at another bar. They send the marines to a bar where they play vintage porn on the walls; the marines go first; when the woman and her friends arrive, there are no marines in the bar. They ask the bartender what happened, and he says that they stepped in, looked around, and stepped out.

She laughs.

It was so funny.

On the Worse Couch

— You look haggard.

— Haggard?

She smirks.

— You know.

— . . .

— Fucked up.

Psychiatrist Check-In

The link's not working.

I refresh the page.

The link's still not working.

I open the page in incognito.

Now the link's working.

— Hey, sorry, the link wasn't working.

— That's no problem. How are you?

— I'm alright, how are you?

— I'm well, thank you for asking.

— . . .

— So, how have your moods been these past few months?

— It's been alright.

— . . .

— A little low lately, but nothing major. Just some work stuff.

— You're still at the-

— Same job, yeah.

— I see.

— . . .

— So, you're happy with the current medication?

— Yeah, I don't think I want to change anything right now.

— And the OCD symptoms?

— It's always kind of the same. But they're manageable.

— If you're interested, we have groups.

— . . .

— I can put in a referral.

— Right . . . let me think about it.

— Of course.

— . . .

— . . .

— . . .

— Should we schedule a follow up then?

— Yeah, let me pull up my calendar.

— It looks like the earliest appointment I have available is in June . . . I have this same time on the 14th, or I can do 2:30, 3, 4:30.

— This time works for me.

— And would you like an email or text reminder? Or both?

— Both is good.

— Great, it's booked. You should receive a confirmation soon.

— . . .

— I'm glad everything is going well.

— Me too.

— Take care.

— You too.

Mushroom Trip to Figure Everything Out

I should get into chores.

Modeling, Second Session

— That wasn't so bad, was it?

— No, not at all. Good time to think.

— Great, well, I'll definitely let you know if we need you to come back.

— Sounds good.

— And here's . . .

— Perfect, thanks.

— Of course. I put in an order with Solidarity Greens this week actually, so I might be seeing you soon.

— Oh nice, yeah, I'll see you soon then.

— Looking forward to it.

Another Friday Night

— You're taking drugs for money now?

— It's a substance, and I feel like that is the least important thing happening here.

— It's a substance that makes movies better.

— It's more than that. It's fucking . . . I can't even explain.
— Evidently.
— Whatever. I'll go again and report back.
— Sure.
— . . .
— . . .
— Anything fun at the synagogue this week?
— Not that I should say.
— Rabbi-congregation confidentiality?
— Something like that.

Another Saturday Morning

— Another black coffee?
— Yeah, that'd be great, thanks.
— And will that be cash or card this time?
— I've got some cash.
— Excellent.
— . . .
— Thank you.
New kind of smile.
Only one person's sitting outside. It's a little cold. But in a nice way.

Third CHARACTER

There's a table and a chair this time. She knocks.
— Come in.
— Thank you.
— . . .

— How are you this week?

— I'm good.

— Any residual effects?

— Not really.

— That's good.

Her left hand is holding a box; her right hand is holding a few pieces of 8.5 x 11 paper. She puts the box on the table and keeps the paper.

— Don't open it until I leave. I will give you more instructions then.

— Okay.

She puts the paper face down on the table and leaves.

The intercom sounds fuzzy.

— Go ahead.

I open the box.

— A ring.

— Yes, we've made a form factor upgrade. Put it on.

I put it on.

— Now twist it.

Fuck that pinches.

— That's how you know it's on.

— . . .

— Go ahead.

I flip over the pages.

— Read please.

City

The park, it's fair to say, is packed: the dogs are frolicking; the people are lounging; the clouds roll lazily through the sky, stopping, every now and again, to change the day's texture—here, some screaming: a man with no shirt is holding a pit bull; someone's on the ground next to him, face bleeding. The man admonishes the pit bull and, as the first responders begin to arrive, acquires layers: a shirt, a hoodie, even denim (acid-washed). They bandage the man. Other cops arrive. Third, fourth, and fifth responders arrive. Onlookers stare, somewhat engaged. But the engagement can only last so long. It's a holiday, after all, and—as people walk through the blankets, hawking psychedelic wares; as the Pomeranians move sinusoidally through the grass; as a beer is finished; another; a spiked ball is dived after, unsuccessfully; three more beers; a radiating sun—one is forced to conclude: it is, in the final analysis, a good day to be at the park.

But now I'm in front of a cream-colored Edwardian, ringing the doorbell: nobody answers—I ring the doorbell again: still, nobody answers: I ring the bell a third time—nothing. I turn to leave and hear my shoe squelch; I look down; there's blood seeping out from under the door. I twist the ring.

Back in the Room

I wait for something to come in over the intercom.
I keep waiting.
— Hello?
A minute passes.
— Hello?
Another minute.
I step out into the hall. There's another room next door.

— Hello?

Nothing.

I look down—dark fingers leak out from under the door. The floor wobbles a little. Fuck this.

A Perfectly Crowded Bus

A man declares himself *too empathic* and then uses the phrase *accidental bukkake*.

I fiddle with the ring.

Six

Hit the right bell this time.

— Hey, delivery from Solidarity Greens.

— Of course, I remember . . . would you mind stepping inside for a minute?

No one's after this.

— Sure. Shoes off, right?

— Yes, please.

Smells nice. Oven's off.

— Have a seat.

— Sure, is everything alright?

What is that look?

— How are you doing?

— I'm alright.

— Good, good.

— . . .

— I have . . . something I'd like to ask you.

— Sure.

— Did she ever discuss her writing with you?
— Sorry?
— Before she was killed.
— Just that she was working on a *weed book*.
— . . .
— Nonfiction, though, if I remember right.
— . . .
— It sounded cool. I don't know more than that. I'm sorry.
— . . .

She looks pained.
— I-
— Were you two sleeping together?
— What?
— Were you fucking?
— I just delivered her weed.
— . . .
— . . .

A different sort of pained.
— I'm sorry to have disturbed you.
— . . .
— But you understand.
— . . .
— We had to know.
— . . .
— Thank you for coming in. Here . . .
That's a lot.
— Sorry again.
— It's alright.

[46]

— We just had to know.
— It's alright.
— Well then, take care.
— . . .
Door's shut.

What was that? Grief? What is with these people? Were we fucking? That explains the girlfriend. All that staring. Why would you- whatever. They just need something to hold on to right now. In a few weeks, they'll forget about this. Forget about me. I'm a service. I am not a part of their lives. This is not my business.

C'mon, you do not need to honk like that. Fuck. When are they going to fix this bike lane?

Cars.

Cars.

Cars.

When are they going to fix cars?

Home now. Someone's parked their truck on the sidewalk. The people walking by make a comment about it.

There's dirt on the steps. The crow must've fucked up the plants again.

Doesn't seem like anyone is home; her door's open; his is too. Maybe I'll get a coffee before dinner.

Should pee.

Peeing.

Peed.

Wallet's still in my pocket. Phone, keys. Shoes are on. Door is closed. Door is definitely closed. Have my keys.

Dogs.

That scaffolding's been here forever.

Dead rat on the ground.

The guy who's always sitting outside at the cafe is sitting outside at the cafe.

It's not that busy in here. The woman this time.

— We're out of drip, can I make you an Americano?

— Sure.

— I'll just charge you for the drip, though.

— Thank you.

New playlist today. A lot of reggae.

The bus bin's pretty much full. Could balance the mug. I'll try not to think about it all crashing down as I walk away.

— Have a good one.

— You too.

School must be getting out: there are a ton of teens at this stop—that one has cat ears and a one-hitter. A few of them are holding skateboards and talking.

— Am I like . . . a different person around you guys?

— Bro's introspecting.

Two of them laugh.

— I'm serious.

— Kind of.

— . . .

— You're definitely a little more comfortable.

— Huh.

— But everyone's like that bro, that's life.

— . . .

— . . .

— Man.

— . . .

— I just want to find a girl and grow together.

— . . .   — Real.

The bus is almost here.

The bus is here.

The bus is crowded. A group of old people with masks sit at the front and chat. Someone's playing videos with no headphones. A beautiful woman holds a box of ceramics. Someone else holds a rug wrapped around a 2 x 4.

All the bars look busy. Guess it's still happy hour.

Sirens. Let's let the fire trucks pass. That's a lot of smoke— weird, wasn't I just . . .

Freaking Out

— Take a breath.
— The oven was off!
— I heard you.
— The oven was off.
— I heard you.

Mantra on the Bus

It's not my business. It's not my business. It's not my business. It's not my business. It's not my business.

First Experiment

I go to my room. I get in bed. I open my laptop and find a movie. I twist the ring. I approach the seated samurai.

— Cut my arm.

— . . .

— Just a light cut.

— . . .

— If you give me your sword, I can do it myself.

— . . .

— Fine.

Outside, it's raining. The streets are empty, except for someone with a cart. I look for a sharp rock and see the samurai watching me from the entrance.

I slice my forearm.

I twist the ring.

I look down. The blood on my forearm fizzles and dissolves. The wound closes up.

It still stings.

Instantly Deleted Email

Subject: *It was nice seeing you . . .*

Second Experiment

— What happened just now?

— I think they're gonna get married.

— No like, to me.

— Girl what.

— Did I go anywhere?

— Are you okay?

— So I was just on the couch like normal?

— Yes . . .

[50]

— . . .

— Are you trying to get into like astral projection or something?

— Not . . . maybe I should've taken a smaller edible.

— Maybe!

New Stop on the Route

I ring the doorbell.

— Oh, hey.

— Hey! How are you?

— I'm alright, yeah, you?

— I'm good, good. Is that the-

— Yep, it's all here. There's a few different strains; we've got Mellow Yellow this week. And since this is your first order with us, we threw in some edibles, also from local farms. These can take a while to hit, so good to be patient.

— Perfect, thank you. Listen, do you have a second?

Not today.

— I've got a few more stops.

— Right, well, nothing that can't wait. I won't keep you. See you next week then?

— Sure, yeah, see you next week.

At the Stop Sign

A kid in a purple octopus costume looks melancholy.

A Couple's Stretching in the Middle of the Sidewalk

I'll go around.

Someone Yells a Slur out the Car Window

His voice cracks, and she snorts.

Third and Fourth Experiments

Missed the bus. The bus stop's empty, and the screen's not working. I check my phone: 13 minutes.

I look across the street, where there's another empty bus stop. It has an ad on the side. A perfectly ambiguous woman is smiling. *What if you only needed one app?* I twist the ring.

— What began as a humble B2B SaaS has since blossomed into a poly-factor, people-focused, multinational organization dedicated to high-agency, action-oriented solutioneering-

I twist the ring. I'm back at the stop.

New text. 10 minutes until the bus comes.

hey sorry i should bail. feeling pretty out of it

I look at the text and twist the ring. I'm at her place. She's on the couch, facing away from me, that red and blue blanket covering everything except for her feet; her laptop's open, and she has her big headphones on. She stares at the laptop. A mug steams on the coffee table next to her. The tea bag's still steeping. I can hear the pop bleeding through her headphones. Looks like she's added a few floating shelves, some new plants too. The pop cuts out, and a video starts: a child is yelling something I can't understand; an adult is laughing. She moves her fingers up the trackpad and goes back to the pop. The song ends. New song. This one has a good bass line. She nods along to it, moving her head side to side a bit. Her feet tap out the beat. I twist the ring.

Back at the bus stop. No new texts; 7 minutes until the bus comes.

Someone with a beard walks up and starts crooning.

— I'm at the bus stop. I'm at the motherfucking bus stopppp-pppp.

Getting on the Bus

— I'm on the motherfucking busssssss.

Getting off the Bus

A few skateboarders are practicing at the stop. One is doing tricks and has just noticed that the other two aren't watching. The second says to the third,

— But it's my bush.

Getting on the Other Bus

That guy has a lot of drumsticks.

In the Living Room

She's on the better couch.

— You're home!

— Yeah, she bailed.

— Sad. Did she give a reason?

— Not really.

— Classic.

— What are you watching?

— Some dumb monster movie.

— …

— …

— Oh, I saw the start of this. How is it?

— Pretty dumb.

— Is the bird cool?

— We've only seen a talon.

— …

— …

— …

— I think I'm giving up. I'll see you tomorrow.

— Good night.

Fifth Experiment

This room has a healthy number of screens, as well as a healthy number of men in military uniforms, with whom the scientists unsuccessfully plead. The screens show scenes of destruction. There are boards with lights and controls.

A hand grips my shoulder.

— Who are you?

I miss a beat.

— I'm with-

Cuffed. He barks into a walkie-talkie,

— I've apprehended another intruder.

[54]

Turning to me,

— How'd you get in here?

— . . .

The lead scientist looks my way. I look at the lead scientist. He grimaces and looks back to one of the military men.

— You can't just bomb your problems away.

— We can bomb whatever we goddamn please.

I'm led out the door and into the hallway.

— Seriously, how'd you get in there?

— . . .

— Piece of shit.

We walk down the hallway in silence. When we turn the corner, we pause to let a man by; he's shepherding who appears to be another apprehended intruder. The intruder looks at me and mouths the word *comrade*.

The military guy jostles me.

— Are there more of you scumbags?

— . . .

— We can make this easy, or we can make-

I twist the ring. I'm back in the living room.

I look out onto the street. A car drives past. Someone's yelling. Another person is walking their dog.

The fridge is making weird noises.

Up Early

I get out of bed. I get dressed. I put my headphones on. I pick an album. I go to the bathroom. I piss. I wash my hands. I brush my teeth. I tap out the three pills. I go to the kitchen.

I swallow two pills and let the third dissolve under my tongue. I put water in the small saucepan. I put star anise in the small saucepan. I put clove in the small saucepan. I put a stick of cinnamon in the small saucepan. I cut some piloncillo off and put it in the small saucepan. I put the small saucepan on the stove and set it to boil. Bubbles start forming. I grind the coffee. Now it's boiling. I dump in the coffee and cut the heat. I cover the small saucepan and wait five minutes. Then I strain the coffee and head to the better couch.

Turned out okay. I sip and look out the window.

Morning gloom.

High of 65.

Yet Another Friday Night

— My parents say hi.

— Tell them I said hi back. How are they doing?

— They're good.

— . . .

— Oh, good news, by the way.

— What's that?

— My sister's pregnant.

— Aw that's great.

— Yeah. They'll all be in town in May. They want to see you.

— I'd love to see them.

— . . .

— . . .

— So-   — Well-

— Go for it.

— How goes the substance testing?

— Over, didn't hear from them again.

— And the modeling?

— Also finished.

— So what are you going to do now?

— Same old, probably.

Sixth Experiment

Home after an uneventful bus ride. The crow's fucked up another plant, and there are a couple packages out front: the upstairs neighbors are still on their trip; I move the packages inside.

She's on the better couch.

— Hey.

— Hey!

— Just grabbing an ashtray.

— Real.

I grab an ashtray and head back outside.

All this dirt. How long's it been? A year? I guess I'll fix the plant tomorrow.

It's nice out here, on the stoop. Peaceful. Bit of wind.

One of the neighbors stands in front of their stairs, staring absent-mindedly across the street. I watch her for a bit and then twist the ring.

It's daytime now, and the cars look different. A kid runs around the neighbor's legs. There are boxes piled at the door.

The kid is yelling,

— Park! Park! Park!

The neighbor looks back at the door, where another woman stands. The woman at the door says,

— They'll be here in 20.

The neighbor says,

— Okay.

The kid yells.

The woman at the door says,

— Should only take an hour.

The neighbor nods, then looks at the kid and says,

— Park?

Now the kid smiles.

I twist the ring. It's night again. The neighbor's gone inside.

It's a little chilly. A self-driving car idles across the street. The door to one of the apartments opens, and a couple steps out. She's wearing a white fur coat and a matching ushanka; he's wearing black jeans and sunglasses. They get in the car; it drives away. Must be headed to a party.

A woman walks her dog.

A couple walks past.

Someone's carrying a surfboard into their apartment.

Another couple.

— She said that?

— That was literally what she said.

— Jesus.

— . . .

— What an asshole.

— Right?

[58]

A bus approaches. It looks empty at first, but as it passes, I see there are a few people inside.

More talking. I look to my right. Two people stand between a tow truck and a parked car. He's trying to sell her a battery. She's trying to get out of the conversation.

Someone comes to look through the recycling.

Another dog.

The wind picks up.

I like the stoop.

Fridge Raid

There's rice.

Back on the Worse Couch

— How's the rice?

— It's good.

She smirks.

— How was the stoop?

— It was good.

— . . .

— I like the stoop.

She smirks again.

— I don't understand how you are still such a lightweight.

Ah. Being weird.

Oops.

— It's a blessing.

— . . .

— . . .

— Do you mind if I watch something?
— Go ahead.
— . . .
— . . .
— Have you seen this?
— No.
— It just came out. It's supposed to be terrible.
— Ooh.

About Nineteen Minutes of *She's a 10, But* (2023)

Mild psychosis.

Seventh Experiment

I make up an excuse and go to my room.

I need to water the plants and clean; there's laundry that needs to be put away. Don't think any of that's going to happen tonight, though. For a tomorrow me.

I stand in front of the mirror. My hair's kind of fucked up. My eyes are red. There's a grain of rice on my hoodie.

I toss the rice grain and stare for a bit longer. Then I twist the ring.

So I'm here.

. . .

. . .

. . .

I'm never getting out of this fucking room.
I twist the ring again.
I get in bed.

Bad Sleep, Part I

3:13.

Bad Sleep, Part II

4:51.

Bad Sleep, Part III

6:07.

Waking Up to Texts

should we go on a fucking HIKE
not now tho. around 11?

Getting Ready in the Living Room

— What made you want to go on a hike?
— I think it's supposed to be good for you.
— A lot of things are supposed to be good for you.
— We'll be busy, then.
She opens the drawer.
— We're almost out of edibles.
— I can get more.
— Thank youuuuuu Solidarity Greens.
— . . .
— . . .
— Do you want milk with yours?
— Yes, please.

— . . . next one's in an hour.
— An hour?
— We could do something.
— . . .
— I don't really know what to do around here, though.
— That's because there's nothing to do around here.
— . . .
— Let's just go to the park.

Back on the N

It's pretty much empty: us and a family, some single women, two guys.
— Hell yeah.
— I'm saying.
— Boys trip to Vegas.
— Boys trip to Vegasssss.
— Let's go.

Deep in the Park

— I am tripping.
— What's up?
— I feel like I just saw that dude.
— . . .
— And him too.
— There are a lot of similar looking dudes in this city.
— That is true.
It's cold in the shade.

Walking Home from the Park

There's a line of cars double parked with their hazards on.
— What do you think that is?
— No clue.
— Weird.
— Yeah.

House News

— Ugh.
— What?
— Look.
The plant's disheveled.
— This fucking crow!
— Have I told you that it like makes eye contact with me?
— Yeah?
— I'll be sitting on the couch and looking out the window, and it'll land, make eye contact with me, and then go for the plants.
— It wants us to know.
— . . .
— Do you have your keys?
— Yeah.
He's back.
— Hey!
— Hey, what were you guys up to?
— Wanted to go hiking but ended up at the park.
— Classic.
He cleaned. Looks nice.

— What have you been up to?
— Surfed a little this morning. Then I got lunch with a friend. Now I'm here.
— ...   — ...
— So ...
— ...   — ...
— I do have some news.
— What's up?   — ...
— I found a new place.
— ...   — Really?
— Yeah, this studio a bit off Market.
— That's cool.   — ...
— Figured it was time, you know.
— When's your lease start?   — ...
— Technically, May 1st.
— ...   — That's soon.
— Yeah, but I have the keys now.
— ...   — ...
— They're going to give me this month prorated. It was the only way I could get this apartment, and it's pretty sick, honestly. So I'll probably start driving some of my stuff over next week.
— Alright.   — ...
— ...
— That's exciting.   — ...
— Yeah, thank you.
— ...   — ...
— Anyways, do either of you have anything going on next weekend? I was thinking I may throw a little kickback.

I look at her.
She looks at me.
— I don't, do you?
— Nope.
— Sweet. I've been thinking it should have a theme . . . how does monochrome sound?
— Like black and white?
— More everyone dresses as a single color.
I look at her.
She looks at him.
He looks at me.
— Yeah?
— Excellent.
He yawns and stretches out a bit.
— Think I'm going to take a nap.
— . . .   — Good luck.

Debrief

— May 1st . . .
— Yeah.
— That's soon.
— Yeah.
— . . .
— One of your girlfriends could move in.
— Ha, ha.
— . . .
— . . .
— I can write something up tonight.
— Thanks.

Lazy Sunday

— So you're a time traveler?

— Sort of.

— Fascinating.

— What do you do for fun here?

— Look at the stars.

— . . .

— That was an attempt at comedy. We do drugs, mostly.

— Space weed?

— *Space weed*?

— Or whatever, I'm sure there's a different name for-

— Nlorp?

— Nlorp.

First Time Smoking Nlorp

— I am afraid it does not always work the first time.

— Ah.

— . . .

— Well, I can come back another time then.

— I look forward to it.

— . . .

— It was a pleasure meeting your acquaintance, time traveler.

— Yeah, you too.

— Until our paths cross once more.

— See ya.

I twist the ring.

Back in my room now. A little dust tendril swings from the ceiling. Should get that.

He's moving stuff around in his room, it sounds like. Nothing from the kitchen. Maybe she's still asleep.

11:38. I could eat something.

Vanity Plate on the Way to the Bakery

YESDIVA

At the Bakery

— Round two?

— Sorry?

— You weren't here earlier?

— Don't think so.

— Huh.

— …

— My mistake then. What can I get you?

— Can I just get one of the spinach croissants?

— Sure.

She shimmies behind her coworker to get it and then shimmies back to hand it to me.

— Here you are. That'll be $4.25.

She flips the screen around.

— Thanks.

I flip the screen back.

— Thanks.

Walking to the Baseball Fields

An old man is giving an old woman a haircut in the middle of the sidewalk. He laughs as he talks to her. Hair gets caught up in the breeze.

By the Baseball Fields

Down the hill and to the right, there's a big group of people playing ultimate. About five teams' worth. Each team has a different colored pinny. Three of the teams are lined up on the sideline, and two are playing. Every point, one of the teams rotates out.

— Must be some king of the hill shit.

— Must be.

I glance to my right. There's a blanket and a woman sitting on it. Next to her, off-blanket, there's a man in a camping chair. His shirt is generously unbuttoned. She's wearing a hoodie. They look about my age.

Someone dives for the frisbee and misses. The other players clap halfheartedly as they reshuffle into position.

There's snacks on the blanket. A grinder. A lighter. He's smoking something. She reaches over and turns the music down—it's jazz.

Two people below and to the left are tossing a baseball. One of them has a much stronger arm than the other, so his friend has to keep running after it, though he doesn't seem to mind.

— It's the human component of the drum!

He's gotten out of the camping chair now and is standing with purpose, sun-lit. She looks nervous.

— You don't mind, do you?

He's looking right at me.

— Sorry?

He smiles.

— Sorry about that.

She has a different sort of smile.

— We're on shrooms.

— No worries.

He sits back in the chair and keeps smiling.

— The human component of the drum.

Getting a Spicy Chicken Sandwich

Two teens at the counter, one teen behind it.

— It's just sauce.

— It's 75 cents.

— It's that serious?

— 75 cents.

— It is not that serious bruh.

He turns around. He's tall. White. Gaunt. Patchy facial hair.

He shakes his head and walks past me. His friend follows.

The teen behind the register smiles to herself.

— Next!

Seven

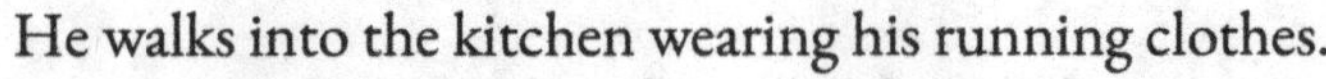

He walks into the kitchen wearing his running clothes.

— Hey.

— Hey.

— Haven't seen you much this week.

— Yeah, it's been a busy week, lots of deliveries.

— . . .

— Next week's 4/20.

— Right, right.

— Done for the day though, and only two tomorrow. So that's nice. How's your Thursday going?

— Oh, not bad, not bad.

— . . .

— I talked to our downstairs neighbors, by the way. We're all set for the kickback.

— Nice. Yeah, I think the upstairs ones are still out.

— Yeah.

He's in front of the mugs.

— Do you mind if I-

— No, no problem.

Kettle's at 178. 179. 180.

— Fuck, you see this?

He's frowning at his phone.

— What's up?

— That woman who got shot? The novelist?

Shit.

— Now her partner's dead too. Same deal. At home, shot in the forehead.

Shit shit shit shit shit-
— Man, that's sad as hell.

Second Time Smoking Nlorp

Shit!

Space Porch

— So, what do you think?
— It's exactly . . . the owls, the crickets . . . everything.
— We can do cicadas as well.
— Wow.
— . . .
— What are the weather options?
— Let us see.
The thunder!
— I think this could fix me.
— Are you broken, time traveler?
I make eye contact. He's looking at me, earnestly.
— Just some . . . you know.
— I do not.
— People keep dying.
— People you love?
— No, more . . . people around me.
— . . .
— Clients, I guess.
— Important ones?
— . . .
— I see.

— ...

— ...

— Are you hungry?

Space Diner

— Select something from the menu, and it will atomically reconfigure.

— Right.

— ...

— Can you search?

— The sum of human culinary expression.

— ... what's in this?

— Space cabbage.

— Do you actually-

He's looking at me again.

— Time traveler.

— ...

— You carry with you an aura of tremendous absence. Did you know this?

— ...

— ...

— Sort of.

— The murders?

I shrug.

— But as you have said, they have nothing to do with you.

— That's true.

He looks out the window.

— Many die.

[74]

— That's true.
— Nevertheless.
— . . .
— . . .
— . . .
— Religious fanatics.
— Sorry?

He gestures to the window. A crowd has gathered around a woman standing on something; she has a sign, but it's in a hieroglyphic language. One of them's an x-ed out pair of eyes.

— It is a cult of religious fanatics. They want to kill our God.
— You have a God?
— Everyone has a God.
— Why do they want to kill yours?
— They claim it will lead to more freedom.
— Will it?
— Who knows.
— . . .
— . . .

He adjusts his space fork.

— This was a good choice.
— Thank you.
— . . .
— . . .
— I hope you find the peace you desire, time traveler.
— I'll try.

One of those impossible smiles.

Theories

— It's a tontine.

— …

— It's a polycule.

— …

— They're not actually dead.

— …

— They themselves witnessed a murder and are slowly being picked off-

— Is this helping?

— …

— …

— No.

— …

— It doesn't matter.

— Yes.

— Who am I to question God's will?

He's amused.

— You believe in God now?

— Everyone does.

He laughs.

— No they don't.

— …

He ashes into the wooden turtle.

— Do you want my advice?

— I would never deprive you of an opportunity for professional development.

— Go back to your life.

— …
— …
Someone's sing-yelling below the balcony.
— Do you hear that?
— They're just drunk.
— …
— …
— Yeah.
— You heard me.
— I did.

New Kind of Bus

This bus is shorter. A woman in scrubs sits near the front and stares out the window across from her. Hard to tell if she's coming from work or going to it. It's like there's condensation in her eyes.

The pair of skateboarders standing near the middle of the bus stumble as it lurches forward. They make eye contact and smile at each other sheepishly.

Ambiance is being provided by the man in the back, who is cradling a boombox that's playing rap I don't recognize. Sounds local. We make eye contact. He scowls.

I wait a few seconds before twisting the ring.

Sitting on the Steps

Living room light's still on.

Severed

She flicks on the lights.
I look up.

Bad Sleep, Part XXIV

4:22.

Nuclear-Strength Iced Coffee

How do they make it this strong? Probably better not to know.

It's mostly empty today. Just the woman who's always reading. Her hoodie has small holes at the top corners of the pocket. A few old people too. A couple.

— No it's insane like they were both murdered in exactly the same way, literally weeks apart.

— Damn.

Outside, it's foggy and cold. I'm the only one sitting there. Maybe today will be different.

Taking the N to the Botanical Garden

Car's deserted. The city rolls by.

At the Gate to the Botanical Garden

An old woman is at the selling table, ringing up two younger women: the one who's not holding the plants is animated, talking about the difficulty of growing plants in the different microclimates; the other one is spaced out but seems happy holding her plants.

The guys two in front of me in line need to pull up their lease to show proof of residence. Behind me are two families, a man, and a couple.

It's foggy here, too.

Exhibition Garden

The guy with cuffed jeans is wearing two hats.

Garden of Fragrance

— No, man . . . I know that . . . I'm telling you I know that . . . I don't give a fuck about her KPIs . . . yeah, and who cares?

Rhododendron Garden

— . . .

— . . .

— . . .

— . . .

The kid takes a sip from his sippy cup and lets out a deep sigh. The dad laughs, genuinely.

— That's a good one. I should try that.

He takes a sip from his water bottle and sighs.

— Cheers.

Mediterranean Garden

Interesting plants.
— That was fucked up of her to say.
— . . .
— It was, dude.
She sighs.
— This slash and burn shit.
— . . .
— Dumb as fuck, honestly.
— Yeah.
— Don't get me wrong-
— I know.
They get up.
— Have you been drawing?
— Not really.
— I get that.
— It'll happen.
— Yeah.
They leave; the guy on his phone shows up.

Path to the Ancient Plant Garden

A woman's wearing big headphones.
The two hat guy.
Some more kids.

Ancient Plant Garden

I look up from the sign, and everyone's gone. I am alone. Plants and shrubs and trees and sounds I've never heard. Bugs. Mud. No platform. My feet are covered.

Something huge flies overhead and blots out the sun. More strange noises.

These must be the residual effects. If it works like the ring, then my body is still in the Ancient Plant Garden. I should be safe, sort of. And what happens if I twist the ring? Something far away shrieks. The air feels different here. It's hard to breathe. Can I die? How many millions of years would have to pass?

A fire truck screams in the vegetation. The sounds of other traffic shift into focus. Something snaps behind me; I turn, but there's no one there. Just the plants and the shrubs and the trees and the mud. Two boot prints. Biggish. Facing me.

When I look back, the sign is there again. A few seconds pass, and I feel my feet on the platform. The mud melts off my shoes in streaks. Two women are standing close by, looking at me, and speaking quietly in French. When I move, they pause.

I need to go home.

Walking Back from the Botanical Garden

Dog.
Dog.
Jogger.
Dog.
Stroller.

Jogger.

Dog.

Two teens smoking at one of the benches.

— You gotta do it . . .

— I know.

— It's good sleep hygiene.

— I know.

Stroller.

Dog.

Someone biking on the wrong path.

Dog.

Walker.

Dog.

Dog.

Walker.

Dog.

Jogger.

Stroller.

Dog.

Dog.

The Kickback

— . . .

— . . .

— Your balcony is so nice.

— Thank you.

— If I had this room, I'd smoke out here all the time.

— You show so much restraint with the stoop.

— …

— …

— Good point.

— Just kidding.

She exhales. We look out into the neighbors' garden for a bit.

— Where's your bling?

— My bling?

— That ring you kept fiddling with.

— Oh right, yeah.

— …

— Got tired of it.

— I liked it.

— …

— Obsidian is kind of in.

— I didn't know.

Behind us, the door slides open.

— Thought I might find you two out here.

— Hey.   — …

— Can I hit that?

I hand him the joint.

— This is such a nice balcony.

— …   — Thank you.

He brings it to his lips.

— …   — …   — Hffff.

— …   — Hffffffffffffffff.   — …

— Hffffffffff.   — …   — …

We finish the joint; he looks happy.

— …   — …   — …

Someone inside is yelling.
— I should get that.
— We'll head in in a bit.   — . . .
— Sounds good.
The door slides shut.
— . . .
— . . .
— . . .
— What do you think we're gonna do?
— About his room?
She shakes her head.
— I mean . . . like . . .
Gestures around.
— Oh.
— . . .
— I don't know.
— . . .
— . . .
She looks at me.
— I feel like you have it figured out.
— . . .
— I was thinking about this after I saw you last night. Sorry if that's kind of a weird thing to say. I just feel like . . . I guess I've only known you for a year, but it feels like . . . like you struggle, yeah, but you know what you want from life, and you kind of just like . . . execute. But like with me I like . . . I don't know . . . I just like . . . I guess I don't know, is what I'm saying. I don't know.
— . . .

— I'm sorry, this isn't making much sense.
— No, you're good.
— . . .
— I get it.
Her eyes look like marbles.
— You're 25.
— Yeah.
— You have a good job.
— Yeah.
— Lots of friends.
— Yeah.
— Lots of lovers.
— That's true.
— . . .
— But I kind of . . .
— . . .
— No, I don't know.
— . . .
— I'm sorry. I'm so high.
— It's okay.
— . . .
— . . .
— . . .
More noises from inside.
— Should we go in?
— I think I'd rather stay out here.
— . . .
— Will you stay too?
— Yeah.

— . . .
— . . .
She smiles.
— It's nice tonight.
— Yeah.
The clouds pass over the moon.

Wake and Bake

There are cups everywhere, in various states. This one is half-full of just dark liquor. Smells like rum. There was ginger beer, wasn't there? Orange juice mixed drink. Coke mixed drink. Gin and tonic? I make an unholy mixture in the sink and start loading the dishwasher, which is half-full from Friday— she put the bowls the wrong way again; we should probably get a new basket. I run it and wait to see what noises it'll make. But there are no weird ones. I leave the rest of the cups and plates in the sink, and, when that's full, a few on the counter next to it. The trash is full. There are three flies. I sweep. Two slices left in the pizza boxes. Don't.

Sticker on the Pole on the Way to the Store

Is humanity worth saving?
Join The Movement.

Another Sight on the Street on the Way to the Store

A man is wheeling a clear plastic suitcase, inside of which is a very small dog.

Back from the Store

She's up and on the better couch now.
— Thanks for cleaning!
— Yeah of course, no problem.
— You doing anything tonight?
— Probably just chilling.
An anticipatory smirk.
— If I don't have a Veggie Combo for 2 and maybe a sambusa, I will die.
— Die die?
Another one.
— Perish.
— . . .
— . . .
— Can I have some of your stuff?
— We'll leave at 7.
— Sure.

Veggie Combo for 2

— But the whole thing is like . . . if you didn't want me to fuck other people, why would you agree to be in a relationship where I can fuck other people? And if you don't want to fuck other people, why did you agree to be in a relationship where you can fuck other people? I truly do not get it. Like there are so many people you could be in a relationship with. This city is teeming. And it's not even like she's crazy insecure, you know? Like she's so self-possessed. *And* she hasn't been monogamous for *years*. These are not experienced gripes.

— For sure.

We'll need more injera.

— . . .

— So, she's not going to be moving in?

— Do you really want that?

— Dunno, never met her.

— That's true.

— . . .

— She's older.

— You've mentioned.

Waitress is here.

— When you're ready.

She drops off the check and leaves.

— I don't remember asking-

— No me either.

— Hmm.

— Yeah.

She glances down at the table. There's a new notification on her phone.

— Ah.

— What's up?

— She heard us.

— What's it say?

— That's kind of private?

— My bad.

— Just kidding. She wants to see me after this. Do you mind?

— Do what you gotta do.

— You know that's what I like about you.

— . . .

— So magnanimous.

— . . .

— Do you want any more or are you good?

— No, we can pay.

She tries to make eye contact.

There's a family to our left. A man two tables down is eating alone and looking at us in the mirror. He looks away when he sees me notice.

The waitress is back to pick up the card.

— Thank you.

Outside, on the Street

She exhales.

— What's up?

— That was good!

— Yeah.

— I live another day.

— Bless.

— Okay!

She claps.

— We need to make some progress on the roommate search this week.

— For sure. I'll respond to some of them tonight, see if they can come by this week.

— Amazing. I'll see you tomorrow then?

— See ya.

She bounces away.

Just missed the train, it looks like. 15 minutes until the next one. Kind of a quiet night. I guess it is Sunday. Couple. Family. Couple. Friends. Family. There really is something about this neighborhood.

Boba place is closed. Isn't there a bookstore around here?

The Bookstore

The sign out front says: *Event in progress. Please be mindful.*

When I walk in, the person behind the register glances up and smiles; there are new releases to my right. I don't recognize any of them. They're mostly hardcover. Never got that. Seems worse.

New Nonfiction. Staff Picks. Small Presses.

Down a few shelves, someone's doing a reading.

— Whence the penis, disassembled.

Scattered applause. It's all adults, but they're sitting in the kids section.

— Thank you. I have two more. I wrote this one a few weeks ago, so it's still kind of fresh. It's called "Another Pussy Poem" . . . ahem . . . respect the trans bereft of plans and sex, I don't. I don't respect myself, oh no! I guess, I guess, I guess, I guess, no flex: I do suspect my hectic mess is flow? I'm lit

on couch betwixt a house betwixt a house, a certain pout af-
fixed my mouth, my gout, I don't have gout, my gout-blessed
piss in bladder bound, *you don't have gout?* ran out, or outh,
I guess, unsure, unbound, I piss on not the couch. I have a
pussy, queen, so hark the sounds of splattered piss, *uh miss?*
amidst this shit a mischievous miss seen, too. Bawdy bitch, I
body bitch, my body is mine not mine is mined not mind qua
me.

Some hesitation, then scattered applause.

— Thank you. This last one is called "Mack" . . . ahem
. . . Mack, A.K.A. That Mad Fat Man, attacks a flapjack stack—
Mack gags: *ack! Al, man, damn!* Al—a small, half-bald, lard
ball—snaps: *Man, Mack! A stack's a stack's a stack, and a
trash act's half-ass clap trap-* Thwack! Mack slaps that lard
ball hard as a czar's law—bar's all slack jaws. *Mack ya whack
cad* barks Art, and Mack's fast arm's an ax that damns Art's
lax alarm—man's hand lands fast, and Art's all salt. As Art
bawls, Mack stands and calls: *Y'all all talk, y'all all stank, y'all
small shafts can't slam a skank. Glam-ass, mad-ass, ya sad
sacks scram at ass-wrapt grams a crank. Ya whack. Crap. Can't
grasp Mack.* And that barb's an all bar brawl spark: hark a
clang, a bat swang, psalms sang, and sharp *dangs* as brash brats
bang gats at rag clad abs: Matt's, Brad's, Ang's. All laws hang
as glass and man fall—at last, at half past, that brawl thaws;
damn, man, a man drawls. Flag's half mast and carcass stank
wafts; bar's rank, a graph, a map: man's wrath. Mack stands
tall as S.W.A.T. vans call, hand grasps a last Pall Mall—Mack
draws. And as S.W.A.T. arms blast at Mack, a mad man's last
act: *What, man? A bad stack's a bad stack.*

Some applause. The moderator introduces the next poet, who's carrying what looks like a large scroll.

Cooking. Spirituality. American History. Used Fiction. Probably wouldn't be in the used. What name would they have it under? No, it's not here—maybe I'll try the new fiction.

Nope, not here either.

— It's not there.

Him.

— Sorry, didn't mean to scare you, just saw you in the back of the reading there, and thought I'd sneak out and say hi.

— Hi.

— . . .

— . . .

— I liked that person's poetry.

— Yeah, it was funky.

— They don't have it here.

— . . .

— But I'm pretty sure you can get it online.

— Right.

— Can't believe both of them . . . so sad.

— Yeah.

The person who was behind the register is standing behind him, looking at us in a way that suggests we need to be more mindful of the event in progress.

— Maybe we should . . .

— Right.

Outside the Bookstore

The guy from dinner is smoking a cigarette across the street.

— Do you want to see some of the paintings?

— Oh, sure.

— You don't have to.

— No, I want to.

— Here, one second . . .

He's finished his cigarette but hasn't moved.

— Here you go.

— It's still-

— Click the side three times.

Color's back now.

— Wow.

— . . .

— These are good.

— Yeah, it's a really talented group this year.

— I like this one.

— Yeah, she really took to it.

— Very, what's the word . . . kinetic?

The guy's still there.

— Can I ask you something?

— Yeah, sure, but do you mind if we start walking?

— No problem. Which way are you headed?

— Just to the stop there.

— Great.

— What's up?

— I was just wondering if you'd come by the studio again.

Not for a class this time. Just thought we should talk.

— Oh, uh-

— There'll be other people around, don't have to worry about anything like that.

Where is he?

— No yeah, that sounds good. When?

— Does Wednesday work?

— Yeah, I can do after like 7?

— Perfect. Let's say 7:30, if that works?

— Sounds good.

— Alright, well, I'm glad I ran into you.

— Same.

— I'm headed that way.

He turns and walks back toward the bookstore.

Nearly Empty Train Car

— Maybe this is just the friend group finally falling apart.

— That'd be sad.

— I don't know.

— . . .

— Maybe it's time.

Monday

The door opens.

— You're back early.

— Surprise all hands invite last night. Attendance *strongly encouraged*.

— Yikes.

— Yep.

— Do you want me to make you a coffee?

— That'd be great.

Kettle's set. Grab the right spoon. 6g. 14g. 21g. 20g. Grind, grind, grind, grind-

— So methodical.

— Ah . . . yeah.

— . . .

— It's a nice ritual.

— I bet.

— How was last night?

— She really bites.

— Cool.

— But we'll go into detail later. What'd you do?

— Not much. Saw a bit of a poetry reading.

— Cool.

Kettle's not close.

— Oh by the way, we have two potential roommates that could come by later. I'm thinking around 6 or 7.

— 7's good.

— 7 it is. I'll tell the first person 7 and the other 7:30.

— What if the first person's late?

— I think we can figure it out.

Kettle's closer.

— How was the poetry?

— What?

— At the reading.

— Oh, it was alright. A lot of rhymes.

— Interesting.

— Also a lot about getting a pussy.

— Ay.

— …

— Speaking of which.

I look at her.

— I have to pee.

Kettle's about there.

Overshot the bloom.

Pour.

Pour.

— I'm back.

Pour.

— It'll drain in a second.

— Thank you.

— I have to head out pretty soon, though, so I'll see you later.

— Thank youuuu.

First Sight Outside

There's a car with an industrial-sized bag of peeled garlic sitting in the open trunk. No driver.

First Delivery of the Week

Huge package on their steps. Furniture?

Doesn't seem like anyone's home. Wish we could just leave it in the mailbox. Have a note here somewhere. *Sorry we missed you*.

So many strollers in this neighborhood. Probably shouldn't then. Maybe I can dip into the park.

That passing car is slowing down and not passing me. One second. Two seconds. Three seconds. The door opens. Someone gets out. Heads the other way. It's speeding up now, going by, passing a teenager running towards me, past me, to the scooters that are locked up a bit behind; his backpack was bouncing the whole time; he looked stressed—what month is it? April? Maybe he's late.

Bike's still there.

Roommate Group Text

Heads up, going to start moving some of my stuff out today

Scooter Update

He's having trouble unlocking it with his phone.

Last Delivery of the Day

— And what should I do if I get too high?

— Try to remember that everything's supposed to feel different.

— . . .

— . . .

— That's it?

— That's really the main thing. Go to a space you feel safe in, lie down, remember that it's temporary.

— . . .

— I will say the Periwinkle in there can be pretty strong, so you may want to start with one of the other strains.

— Okay.

— . . .

— Well, thank you.

— Of course.

Shuts the door. The woman on the street glances up from her phone. She hasn't moved at all.

Roommate Update

She comes out of her room a minute or two after she hears me open the door.

— Hey!

— Hey, how was your meeting?

— So dumb.

— Yeah?

— They've announced . . . *The Regrowth Initiative*.

— What's that?

— That's what everyone's asking. They didn't say anything concrete they were literally just like *everything's going to change*.

— . . .

— So layoffs.

— That's stressful.

— Yeah, people were freaking out. It's so stupid.

— Yeah.

— How was your day?

— Busy. 4/20 week. A lot of new people.

— *Try to remember that everything's supposed to feel different.*

— Exactly.

— OH, can't believe I forgot, go look in his room.

— Is he here?

— Go look.

I left my light on.

It's totally empty.

— Did he-

— Fully moved out.

— Wow.

— Like left the key on the counter and everything.

— Did he say anything?

— He was like, *Oh I'm sure I'll see you guys soon.*

— Weird.

— And then he left!

— Weird.

— . . .

— Maybe I'll text him.

She laughs.

— What?

— Nothing. Is the person still coming at 7?

— Yeah.

— Sweet.

First Potential Roommate

The way he's looking at her.

Second Potential Roommate

— I mean like being a roommate *as* a practice.

— ...   — ...

—Which is what I think we should foster.

— ...   — Word.

Comparing Notes

— Yeah.

Tuesday

Up early. Need a coffee. Need a morning walk, too. It's wet outside. Gray. The fog's there somewhere. Yesterday was trash day: permutations of green, black, and blue all along the sidewalk. I get to the crosswalk, look left, look right—there's the fog, hanging over the trees up the hill, in front of the pink house.

Something about this music doesn't feel right; I take out my headphones and stuff them in my pocket.

Better. Sounds of steps. Keys jingling. A man with a baby strapped to his chest passes by. A woman comes down a fire escape holding a mug of coffee. The corner store has a rainbow flag taped to the inside of its window using beige masking tape. A young woman crosses the street wearing white noise-canceling headphones and the same green pants that I'm wearing; she's also holding a coffee. Howling. Up a street, on the other side, there's a small encampment. A booted foot hangs out of the blue tent. A woman howls in the red one. Some people stand on the nearby steps, staring. A man stands in front of the grated corner store, smoking a cigarette and watching. In front of me now is a man in a tank top with an unleashed dog he's calling *princess*—he has a butterfly tattoo on his left calf and a moth on his right; arrows peek out the tops of his purple socks; his neck hair is textured. The light ahead just turned green. Might make it in time. Someone's left a scratched leather recliner on the street. No room for it. A cop car drives by with its lights on but no sirens. I make the light. At the bus stop, a teenager picks his nose and a short old woman with a mask stares at him. A stunningly loud flock of pigeons takes flight, and a straggler pigeon struggles to catch up with them. An abandoned sticky note near the school says *MATTH*. A woman in pink running clothes holds two coffees. Her top matches her shoes. Her shoes match her hair tie. She smiles when we make eye contact.

I turn around near the cafe, which is open but basically empty. Trash day up here too. Three blue recycling bins next to one another. A car with a logo I don't recognize. I guess they must make new cars. I'm not going to make the light.

Waiting for the Green Light

The sounds of all the passing cars slick together into a single wet rope.

Another Morning Surprise

When I open the door, she's making coffee.
— Walk?
— Yeah.

— Anything good?

I shrug.

— Someone else is coming by today at 7.

— Okay! I'll be here.

— . . .

— I don't know if you saw, but he sent us a long text. *Ended up moving everything out, but I wanted . . .*

— He was kind of a weird guy.

— Yeah.

A headache's starting. Day of deliveries still ahead.

Fourth Delivery of the Day

Head's still hurting.
Two cats leering at her feet.
At least it smells nice.

New Roommate

— Yeah, I do customer support for this AI company. Mostly answering emails all day. Pretty stupid. Most of our customers just use it to make hentai.

— . . .   — Nice.

— Yeah.

— . . .   — Been there long?

— Yeah, second year? Money's alright. Work's pretty easy. Paid for my surgery. Lets me focus on other stuff.

— . . .   — What sort of stuff?

— Music, mostly.

— . . .   — What sort of music?

— I guess it's a bit like ambient.

— . . .   — Sick, I've always wanted
                                          to get into ambient.

— Yeah.

— . . .   — . . .

— Textures.

— . . .   — Word.

She looks at me.

— So . . .

— Right, so what would your timeline be like?

— I can move in whenever. Ideally it'd be in the next couple of weeks? I'm month-to-month.

— Cool, yeah, I mean . . .

We make eye contact. She nods.

— We-   — You-

— Go ahead.

— Yeah, no I mean, I think you'd be good to move in as soon as you want. You could start paying rent in May, since our old roommate's already paid for this month. I mean right that's if you're interested, but-

— Definitely.

— Great, well, we'll talk to the landlord about getting you on the lease, then.

— Cool.

— . . .   — . . .

— . . .

— . . .   — . . .

— So like, should I-

— Later this week, once we've talked to the landlord and got the lease sorted out, you can come by and pick up the keys?

— Cool, cool.

— . . .

— Alright, well, I'll wait to hear about the lease, and we'll see from there?

— Perfect.

— Cool.

He closes the door.

She waits a bit.

— Ambient boyyyy.

— Yeah.

— This is going to be so good.

— Hope so.

Wednesday

The encampment's been cleared.

Third Delivery of the Day

— Yeah, this week's special is the Periwinkle. It's strong, but it's fun.

— Groovy.

At the Worst Four Way Stop in the City

There's no way they didn't see me in the crosswalk.
There's no way.

At the Studio

It's been like five minutes.
Voicemail again.
Street's empty.
Voicemail again.
Ten minutes.
Car drives past.
Did he forget?

Grabbing an Ashtray

— Hey.
— Hey! You got a package.
— Thanks.

Sitting on the Stoop

It's not hitting.

Holiday

The femme one is holding the butch one; her hair is red and blazes in the sun. They sit in the garden below and watch as people below them parade by in their costumes: an 80s exercise video is moving past, at the front of which is a girl in a blue leotard, which sparkles as she pulls too hard on a vape, starts to cough, recovers, hands it to the boy in mismatched legwarmers, purple and orange legs only a few paces ahead of the next group, which is going for something cyberpunk, their hair spiked, their sunglasses on, overheating, probably, in all the leather; there are frat boys dressed as a different era of frat boy; there are other kinds of leather; there are people doing something reflective. The femme one scratches the butch one's head. The cigarette smells warm and feels good in my lungs. It's a perfect day, of course, because what else would it be? The sun is there but gentle, like the clouds, like the breeze, like the trees, like their leaves, like their fluttering, like the world exhaling; everything feels alive, real. Now the butch one is holding the femme one, pointing at the plane flying overhead, undeservedly mundane. The femme one murmurs; she's started rolling a joint, packing it down with a chopstick—when she's finished, they smoke it together in silence.

But it wouldn't have been like that. Not for me. I twist the ring. I'm back holding the book. My mirror's still dirty. My laundry's still there. The little dust tendril's still there. I'm still here. This is life. This is what being alive is.

Mid-Afternoon Coffee

At the good table, a youngish man stares at his computer with his headphones in.

— Right . . . right . . . well yes, but . . . right . . . right . . . no, I mean you're right.

One table over.

— But like if we go out.

— Then we're going to go out.

— Exactlyyyyy.

Someone's yelling at the corner across the street.

Another regular's here now; the barista gossips. After he orders, she picks up the electric fly swatter, and the cafe comes alive with zaps.

Long Afternoon Stroll

Feels short.

Late Afternoon Surprise

She's sitting on the stoop.
— How was the beach?
— Look inside.
— What-
— Just look inside.
No dirt on the steps.
The upstairs neighbors took their packages in.
What the fuck?
— Did you leave the door open?
— I definitely closed it.
— …
— Like very sure.
— …
— Maybe the upstairs neighbors left it open?
— They fucked up your room pretty bad.
Oh what the fuck.
— They went through my room too, but they didn't take anything. Like neither of my laptops. Nothing.
— …

Nothing's missing from the kitchen either. And it doesn't
like they took anything out of your room.
— There's honestly not that much to take.
— …
— …
— What do you think they were looking for?
Fuck.
— No idea.

Friday

— You had yesterday off?
— Yeah.
— Did you do anything special?
— Not really.
— …
— Very regular day.
— I see.
— How was your week?
— Very regular.
— …
— Very rabbinical.
— …
— Are you good?
— Yeah.
— …
— Why?
— You seem elsewhere.
— Just, you know …

— . . .
— High.
— Of course.

Standing at the Bus Stop

The man on the other side of the street did not get on that bus.

Reading on the Bus

Let us set the scene: it is late; it is Tuesday; in another world-

Epiphany

It's the story!

Shabbat, Part II

He opens the door.
— Are-
— It's the fucking story!
— What?
— The story, the fucking story, the one they had me read at the the CHARACTER study. It's *her* story. She wrote it. It's about me. That's why they, all the fucking . . . looks, all the attention, the the like *are you fucking her* interrogation. It's about me! She was writing about me! And the fucking CHARACTER-
— What is CHARACTER?
— The substance!

— I thought you were done with that.

— No you're not listening, she must've had some too! And then, I don't know, she fucked something up, and that's why there's another me walking around-

— What are you talking about?

— The fucking, it all, like-

— Do you feel safe?

— What?

— Are you having an episode?

— No I'm trying to tell you-

— Trying to tell me what.

— What?

— I fucking can't, alright?

— Can't what?

— I wait for you to show up at my door and do something exactly like this.

— What are you talking about?

— You don't see yourself.

— . . .

— You need to see yourself.

— What are you talking about?

— You have a life! A life that you are throwing away-

— I'm not throwing anything away.

— . . .

— My life is fine.

— Your life is stasis.

— That is all anyone wants.

— Yeah, and how is that going?

— What?

— Do you think people are happy? Fulfilled? Do you think this is the life they want to live? Weren't you a communist? You're allowed to want more from your life than stability.

— I-

— And stable? You're high every-

— *You're* going to lecture me about getting high?

— I'm not you!

— What?

— . . .

— . . .

— Fuck.

— . . .

— Get out of my apartment.

In the Stairwell

I'm not you!

Outside

— You were basically right.

She—the other me—is standing by the door.

— I have a gun, and I will shoot, so don't-

I tackle her, and she vaporizes. The gun hits the ground but doesn't go off. Her clothes fall with it.

No one else is on the street. One of the self-driving cars goes past.

I should change.

Turning the Corner

Modeling guy?
— And?
— . . .
— You got the ring, I see.
The CHARACTER is speckled with white now.
— Yeah.
— Good. Give it to me.
I give him the ring. He looks at the poster across the street and twists it.
He twists it again.
— Nothing. Must be dead.
— Must be.
— I'll tell the others.
— Right.
He hands me the ring.
— No witnesses?
— None.
— Good. You're one of the infiltrated now.
— . . .
— It's been easy enough so far. Just act natural. No one will notice a thing.
— Right.
— We'll be in touch.

Home, by the Knives

Don't.

Some Attempts at Much-Needed Sleep

2:47. 3:13. 3:14. 3:15. 3:42. 4:00.

Eighth Experiment

It still works.

Breakfast

— You look tired.
Why's she up?
— Long night.
— . . .
— . . .
— Did you talk to the landlord, by the way?
— Yeah, someone's coming by to change the lock today.
— Great.
— And then he can come pick up the keys tomorrow.
— Great.
— . . .
Coffee's almost done.
— Can you make me one too?

Space Database

— Nothing?
— My apologies. We have no record of a substance called
CHARACTER.
— I guess that makes sense.
— . . .

— …
— …
— Could we like … scan it or something?
— Surely.
He takes out what looks like a barcode scanner and points it at the ring.
— Intriguing.
— What?
— It does not appear here, either. This substance is not native to our universe.
— …
— Very intriguing. I will do some research.

Text Sent a Little After Sundown

can we talk?

Texts Received Soon After

Sure.
You can come over around 9.

Saturday Night

He opens the door, and we sit on the couch.
— So.
— I'm quitting weed.
He looks at me but says nothing.
— For a few weeks, at least.
— …

— I want to see what my life's like without it.

— That seems wise.

— . . .

— . . .

— I don't know why I thought you would be happier.

— You've only decided to change.

— Can you drop the rabbi schtick for like half a second and just talk to me like I'm your friend?

— This is how I talk to my friends.

— I will actually leave.

He smiles.

— I'm happy for you. Genuinely.

— Thank you.

He smiles again.

— But where am I going to find a new Shabbos stoner?

— You're a ridiculous person, you know that?

— Why do you think I became a rabbi?

— To fuck with me, specifically.

— That too.

— . . .

— . . .

— I'll still come by.

— I know.

— . . .

— How will you fill the rest of your time?

— I don't know.

— . . .

— Thought I might try to get back into reading?

— That sounds fun.

Sober Bus Ride

A guy licks his fingers, then rubs the stamp on the back of his right hand.

Next to him, someone says into the phone, *it's about me haircut. A fooking disaster*. It looks alright, though.

Empty House

Her door's open, and she left the light on; there are clothes everywhere; it still smells like vape.

I turn off the light.

Getting Into a Book on a Sunday Morning

— But yours *is* a curious countenance.

— That's the problem.

They exchange a conspiratorial look and giggle. The younger one turns to me.

— Now we must confess something to you.

— Sure.

— In your knapsack-

The older one laughs.

— In your knapsack, there is a tin-

The older one laughs again.

— You must stop!

The younger one turns back to me.

— While you were in the privy, we discovered a tin of confections.

Ahh. Forgot I had edibles.

[116]

— And by that look of recognition, I am to believe you have grasped our current predicament.

— Intimately.

The older one cackles.

— The ball!

The younger one looks genuinely terrified.

— I had forgotten about the ball.

— When's the ball?

The older one waves her hand.

— Imminently. Come. You'll need a dress.

In the Carriage

This ride, it must be said, is irredeemably bumpy.

The Ball

— And this one?

— *An estate of some eleven thousand pounds a year. An agreeable face. An agreeable demeanor. A man known to be pleasant, sprightly, and above all else, shall we say, agreeable.*

— Oh, but you mustn't!

— *Eleven thousand pounds a year.*

They giggle.

— And who should be approaching our very table?

The agreeable man is here.

— Good evening.

— Quite.

The younger one bites her lip. He looks bemused.

— Yes, well, one can't help but notice that it is a marvelous occasion, tonight.

— Very much so.

— And yet if one is permitted to venture a mild criticism, or, perhaps, even a suggestion, it would be that if there is a ball in which two of the most handsome women there find themselves sequestered away from the dancing, then there is, one should think, an opportunity.

— Indeed!

He smiles.

— In that case, may I have the honor of soliciting a dance?

— Oh, I can't help but agree!

The younger one covers her mouth, and the man glances at her.

— But is she well?

— Yes, yes, I feel positively sprightly!

The older one lets out a tremendous snort. The now vexed man looks at me. I smile at the sisters and twist the ring.

Standing in Front of the Mirror

The dress melts away.

Grabbing a Snack

She's on the better couch, making faces at one of her girlfriends. They stop when they see me walk into the room.

— She emerges!

— Sorry?

— Haven't seen you all day. What were you doing in there?

— I was reading.

She laughs.

— I can never read when I'm high.

— I'm sober.

— On a Sunday?

— On every day now.

She laughs again.

— Cool.

New Roommate Question

alright if i come in like 30?

Handing Off the Keys

— This one is for the inside door, and that one is for the outside door.

— Word.

— Do you know when you'll be moving in?

— Probably like . . . Tuesday?

— Sounds good.

Sunday Night Reflection

There's so much extra time.

Going to Work

There's a flattened head of broccoli lying in the street.

Coming Home from Work

There's some cops and an ambulance, a bunch of people standing around—looks like a pretty bad crash. But I shan't linger.

New Book

Snow churns in great volitant eddies; clouds bar bleached moonlight from icicled trees;—it is dark, and the street is nigh deserted: only a few inn signs batter in the imperious wind; all else is frozen still, or soon to be. It is, as any traveler knows, on such a night that an inn door can feel heavy in the hand, it being impossible to know whether you will be stumbling into manifest revelry, or simply intruding upon hollow despair— tonight, manifest revelry it appears to be;—this inn teems with life: here a pack of men in half-thawed furs make inscrutable gambles with dice and cups carved from pale bone; there a slumped drunk is roused by an affectionate slap to his back; in the shadow of a large, decaying spine, other men ribald; everywhere it is pungent.

    — You there, what'll it be?

    — Just water would be great.

    — …

    — …

    — Here you will not find just water.

    — Oh, I-

    — Water cold and unforgiving, yes; magisterial, to be sure; cruel, to be surer. But-

    — Can I get a coffee then?

— Aye.

— Thanks.

I take a seat.

— Your coffee.

— Thank you.

— . . .

— I'll close out at the end of the night.

A man farther down gives a weary signal, drawing him away and sparing me any further conversation; I am left pensive in my thoughts, until the door opens again, and the savage blade of an aeolian scythe cuts through the inn.

— Brothers!

One of the gambling men rises.

— Not here, lunatic.

— Hear me out, at least?

— Aye, like the last nights. And the nights before them. You've come to speak of the Divine Author.

— . . .

— And what do you know of the divine?

He bangs his mug on the table.

— Of war?

The lunatic pulls off one of his gloves. He has a ring.

Back in Bed

Shit.

Quickly Composed Text

the ring's working again

Somewhat Delayed Response

We heard.

Follow Up Text

Wait for instruction.

Sleeping Trouble

3:12.

Wake and Walk

Trash day again: the recycling bins are strewn; they haven't taken the trash or the compost. A woman in interesting jeans jots something down on her phone; the flattened head of broccoli is still lying in the street; two motorcycles approach, side by side, and don't really stop at the four-way stop, where a car has just lurched—once the motorcycles pass, it accelerates to compensate. The old man is washing his car with a hose, and suds go down the sidewalk, past the anarchy symbol;— shit: the flies scatter as I step around. The bus stops, and no one gets on, and no one gets off, and a man carrying a bike on one shoulder up the stairs to his apartment ignores the box of records someone's left out front: funk, soul; the slip that says *FREE* has drifted a few feet up the block, and the tape at the top has folded in on itself, like a little hat. Three parking cops drive by in a line, their lights all flashing. A woman who's taller than she looked coming down the street drums a beat as she waits at the light, which turns green, prompting a honking war; it's still going by the time I'm at the next street, where a man is wearing a hoodie that says *corduroy killer*; a man gets out of the AAA truck, and the corduroy killer shakes his hand and says something to convince the man getting out of the AAA truck that he's older than he is. Doesn't sound like it worked. Someone waiting for the bus is wearing a lanyard. The old ladies are smoking again. Kids and parents mill about outside the school.

I walk back on the other side so I'm not looking into the sun. When I get back, his U-Haul is already there.

— Hey.

— Hey.

— Let us know if you need any help.

— Think we got it, but thanks.

— No problem.

There's a brown thing at the top of the cactus, woollike. Maybe it'll bloom this year. *Solo un día al año.* Funny what you remember.

Eavesdropping in the Coffee Shop

Was she always British?

New Roommate, First Night

— …	— …	— Hffffff.
— …	— Hfffff.	— …
— I'm good.	— …	— …
— …	— …	— Hffffffffff.
— …	— Hfffffffffff.	— …

— …   — …   — Hfffff.
— …   — Hffffffff.   — …

She didn't get much. Must be dead.

A Few Minutes After an Hour and Fifty Six Minutes of *From Where the Mud Flows* (1973)

— I don't think I got it.
— I don't know if it's about getting.
— Tea.

Routine Delivery

— Thanks.
— No problem.

Roommate Reminder

— Don't forget we have the concert Saturday.
— I won't.

Shabbos Stoner

— I don't know. Pretty boring. But fine, generally, I guess. How are you?
— How am I?
He laughs.
— I'm good, thank you for asking. I had a good week.
— What happened?
— Nothing in particular.
— …

— Sometimes the work just hits.
— I bet.
— Can you pass me that?
I pass him the wooden turtle.
— Thanks.
He knocks out more than just ash.
— I had a strange dream last night.
— What happened?
— I was a lawyer.
— . . .
— . . .
— And?
He looks at me.
— It's a very different life.
— . . .
— . . .
— . . .
— . . .
He grins.

Bus Stop Detail

Someone left two identical wigs.

Ring Observation

It's getting whiter.

Better Couch Discovery

New stain.

Waiting for the Bus to the Concert

A young dad stepping into the crosswalk lets go of the stroller so that it rolls down, and then up, the dip, where he catches it. A woman tries to put her hand in a hoodie pocket that doesn't exist. *I don't know why he's trying to text me . . . 45, that's the crazy thing . . . right, that's what I'm saying . . . I know!* Bus is here.

Waiting for the Opener

— Do you want anything?
— I'm good, thanks.
— Be right back then.
A real diversity of outfits here tonight.
Some guys on stage.
Some guys on their phones.
Two of the most beautiful women I've ever seen.
Some old people.
Another beautiful woman.
Great hair.
Great hair.
Talking about work.
Mic check.
The bassist's on stage now.
— Back.

Waiting for the Headliner

— Am I wrong?
— You're not wrong.
— I know.
— . . .
— He had a slutty tattoo.
— . . .
— And a whore's mustache.
— . . .

Still Waiting for the Headliner

— What time was she supposed to go on?

Eight

One of the venue people comes out on stage.

In the Exiting Crowd

— *Medical emergency . . .*
— . . .
— Wonder what it was.
He's here.
— No idea.
Looking ahead. Hasn't seen me yet.
— I'm going to the bathroom.
— Can't it wait?

In the Line for the Bathroom

— That's so sad.
— I know.
A little further up.
— What?

Sticker in the Stall

> *Is humanity worth saving?*
> *Join The Movement.*

Waiting for the Bus from the Concert

After a minute or two of texting, she looks up from her phone.
— I think I'll take the 5 actually.
— Alright.
— ...
— Which one is it tonight?
— ...
— ...
She looks back at her phone.
A few beats.
— I wonder-
— Why are you so dismissive?
— What?
— Of me, of being poly.
— ...

— I don't get why it's such a joke to you.
No one else at the bus stop.
— . . .
— Like it's fine if it's not for you.
— I-
— But it's my life.
— I know.
— . . .
— You're right.
— . . .
— I'm sorry.
— . . .
— . . .
— But like why. Like do you actually have a problem with it?
— No, not at all.
— What is it then?
The bus is a few blocks away.
— Your bus is-
— Girl I don't care about the bus. I'll miss the bus. We're talking.
— . . .
— . . .
— You're right.
— . . .
— I don't know. I'm sorry, I honestly don't.
— . . .
— And I'm sorry I was dismissive. I'll try to be more considerate about it in the future.

— …
The bus is here.
She doesn't get on.
— …
— …
— Is there something you do take seriously?
— …
— …
Staying alive.
— I don't know.
— You should know!
— …
— …
— …
— …
— …
Another bus is a few blocks away.
— You're right.
— …
— …
— …
— You're right.
— I know.
My bus is here.
— Aren't you going to get on?
— Another one will come.
— …
— …
The bus leaves. A man across the street is watching us.

[130]

— . . .
— . . .
— . . .
— . . .
The man is still watching us.
She pulls out her vape, hits it, and offers it. I wave no.
What feels like a minute passes.
— Are you actually going to stop smoking weed?
— I don't know.
— You might need to get a new job.
— Yeah.
— . . .
— Probably.
She checks her phone. I check mine.

One New Text

It's time. We're moving forward.

End of Conversation

She looks up from her phone.
— Next one's delayed. Won't be here for 20.
— . . .
— Think I'm just going to take a Lyft.
— Alright.
— I can add a stop?
— It's alright.
— . . .
— Thanks, though.

The man's gone. Someone else is at the stop now. Older woman. She has one of those carts. Lots of white, translucent bags.

Some Stops Later, on the Nearly Empty Bus

The man at the front talks at the driver about an imminent race war.

The woman across from me smells like smoked salmon.

I look at my phone. Nothing.

Thinking on the Stoop

It's true.

On a Train

I sit somewhere near the back of the dining car, staring out at the large expanse of countryside, where there is nothing to see but snow, and the sun reflected in the snow, and the snow glimmering in the sun, and the bits of my breath still visible in this train car, where it is cold, despite the fact that, using a bit of foresight, and some cunning, I have managed to acquire a large coat.

— It surprises me that a man such as yourself is capable of repeating these falsehoods.

— Falsehoods! You insult me.

The two men sitting in front of me are the only people in the dining car. The one I can see has a curious appearance, that of a man facing a very strong wind: his hair pulled back, his nose upturned, his eyes pulled back, his mouth taut. I cannot see the face of the other man, though I can imagine, based on the way that he speaks, that he is a man of ruddy cheeks, beady eyes, an unkempt, slovenly mustache, and teeth stained by an unrestrained love of tobacco.

— Falsehoods . . . do you think I do not understand why one would believe such things? Do you think I do not understand what compels my fellow man? What blinds them? Of course I understand! It is the beyond. There is no human invention greater than the beyond! For thousands of years, we have been driven by absence. What we have not. And you speak to me of falsehoods! There is nothing more false than this, my friend, the belief that what we desire is right around the corner, there, in the beyond, just outside of our grasp. That we can grasp it. That we can hold it. No, you will not hold it. It will melt in your hands like snow on a warm spring day. You think that what you desire is something, but what you desire is no less than desire itself: this is the God you pray to, the God you sacrifice to, the God you think about each and every day. Absence! Want! Desire! What we have not. You think this because you are living in the beyond. Falsehoods! You say it is I that believes in falsehoods, and yet, when you wake up, and you rub the sleep out of your eyes, you find yourself looking to a world that is not there, a world in which you will never belo-

— So you are an atheist? Or worse still, a nihilist!

— A nihilist! Oh, how you insult me! You stand before me on this very train and tell me that I am a nihilist, that I believe in nothing—I believe in man, my dear friend, man!

How do you think it is that we move through the countryside like this? How do you think it is that we have chairs to sit on, and food to eat, and tobacco to smoke, and ideas to discuss? Do you think these things simply fell here? Do you think that the world you were born into, the world you live in, that it was always there? No! Where you see the hand of God, I see the hand of man. Where you see your tobacco pouch, your pipe, and your match, I see nothing but man, man's hands, man toiling in the fields, man poised above the wood—it is man who made this world, and wherever you go in it, wherever you find yourself, even in the darkest, most desolate landscape you can imagine, in the barren wilderness, where nothing grows, and no one shouts, you shall find man there, too. For you shall be there, you! It is not I who believes in nothing. It is you who has staked your life on what is not here, what exists in the beyond. It is you who has denied the very world that we live in! You are the one that clings to nothing, clings to it as if your very life depended on it.

— If what you say is true, then all-

The door to the dining car opens, and the two men briefly suspend their conversation to observe the new man, who walks right past them and sits next to me, where he removes a glove and reveals a ring.

— We can talk here.

The men resume their argument.

— There have been . . . developments.

— . . .

— Someone is leaking information. They know where we're going to be, and they know when we're going to be there. They know what we're doing. They know why we're doing it.

— ...

— Are you being watched?

— Not that I know of.

— ...

— ...

He sighs.

— Fuck.

— ...

— Did you tell anyone you were here?

— No.

— Good.

— ...

He faces me.

— We're going to have to see who we can trust.

He twists his ring and disappears from the train car. The arguing men haven't noticed a thing.

Trip to the Living Room

He's full spread on the better couch, not wearing very much besides a pair of big headphones; he looks up when he sees me come into the room.

— Shit dude.

— What's up?

— That is a vintage coat.

Coat?

— Really goes with your ring.

Coat!

Ninth Experiment

It's not disintegrating.

Tenth Experiment

It's not disintegrating!

Ethical Considerations

Don't be stupid.

Bank Heist

— Who the fuck are you?
— Just need like five of these.

Different Bank Heist

— Who the fuck-
— Don't worry about it.

Search History, Several Bank Heists Later

price of gold
*1989.67 * 10 * 25*
sell gold near me

Celebratory Afternoon Coffee

I stop dancing when she walks in.
— Oh, don't stop for me.
She pours some water into her mug, pauses a moment, and then decides not to refill the pitcher.
— Girl what is that smile?
— Nothing.
She narrows her eyes.
— Are you smoking again?
— No, no, just . . .
— . . .
— Life is beautiful.
She laughs.
— Happy Sunday.

Talking with the Boss

— Yeah no, pretty regular week this week. One no show today, but I'll head back tomorrow.
— Excellent. And people seem pleased?
— Oh for sure, I think the Periwinkle was a hit.
— Good, good.
She looks at me over her desk.
— So, that's one update down.
— . . .
— . . .
— I wanted to let you know that I will be, that I think . . .
No emotion.
— I think I need to quit.

— . . .

— I stopped smoking and, I don't know, I think I need to do something else with my life for a while.

One second.

Two seconds.

Three seconds.

— Well, this is unexpected. You've been with us a while.

— Yeah I mean, you know I like this job.

— I do.

— It's just . . .

— I understand.

Smiling now.

— This is great news.

— It is?

— It's a pain in the ass for me, of course, but for you.

She extends a hand across the table.

— It's been a genuine pleasure. I hope that you find what you're looking for on this new path. Please come back any time.

— Thank you.

Sitting on the Worse Couch

— Helloooo?

Watching me.

— What's up?

— Really?

— What?

Eyeroll.

Sitting Outside the Coffee Shop

A guy in the crosswalk sees someone he knows and daps them up, a girl walking by tries to rip off a concert bracelet, someone at the bus stop has their Clipper card already out, that cat's in a backpack, that skater's walking, that person's going to bring their dog on the bus, she didn't close the door to the cafe when she went out and she doesn't jaywalk until the light turns yellow and then she jaywalks, goes to the other side of the street, and walks into one of the stores, and this guy's carrying a guitar and talking to his friend about how he's never used a credit card and says *it's evidently bugging me* and walking past and now the people next to me are getting into it about the JFK assassination and the people next to them are signing to each other and laughing and signing to each other and laughing and they seem so happy.

Lying

— I think I'm going to quit my job.

— Really?

— Yeah I don't know with the weed and I got another job offer this week.

— Woah.

— . . .

— What is it?

— Oh we have this old client who's a big like antiquer and I was delivering to her and we were chatting a bit and it turns out she's looking for someone to *help out*.

— . . .

— Honestly for what it is the pay's definitely good enough and the hours are pretty flexible.

— I see.

— . . .

— And you're excited about it?

— Yeah I mean it's not weed and the way I'm thinking about it it's just something I can do while I think about my next move.

— Your next move.

— Exactly yeah.

— Reminds me, my parents and sister will be in town next week. Would you want to get dinner with them?

— Yeah I'd love to see them.

— Great, how's next Thursday?

— For sure let me just put it in my calendar.

— . . .

— . . .

— . . .

— . . . hype!

— Hype.

Walk to the Bus Stop

He's been walking behind me for a few blocks but now he's crossing to the other side of the street and the car ahead of me is pulling out of the parking spot as soon as it sees me coming up and there's a few empty parking spots ahead and a new car is pulling into one of them as soon as it sees me walking up and a new car is pulling into the driveway in front of me but it's only reversing to turn around in the middle of the street and the car is going by and the car is going by and the trees are there and there's someone in front of me who I'm going to have to pass and the footsteps behind me are getting faster and faster and faster and faster and the person passes me and they have a backpack and the car on the other side of the street just turned its lights on and now it's pulling out of its parking spot and there's a guy smoking a cigarette at the corner and he looks at me and I look at him and I look left and I look right and I cross the street and he's still there smoking his cigarette and looking at me and I look behind me and he's gone.

Remembering Something at the Bus Stop

Weren't you a communist?

Thinking on the Bus

Weren't you a communist? Weren't you a communist?

Space Disappointment

— I am afraid I cannot let you take any of it. Any and all interchronological technology transfer is expressly forbidden. The punishments are draconian.

    — ...

    — Besides, without a sufficient energy source, it's useless.

    — What about like documents?

    — Documents?

    — Research?

    — Ah.

A sad smile.

    — I'm afraid not.

    — ...

    — Speaking of, however, I've been looking into your CHARACTER.

    — ...

    — Information is scarce, but I sense that I am close. Perhaps in a few days, I will have something.

Checking the Time

4:44.

Messages

You're drawing attention.
Don't forget the mission.

Checking the Time, Again

5:57

Crashed

They're both in the living room when I come in.

— Long night?
— ...
— ...
— You look terrible.
— ...
— Thanks.
— Don't mention it.
— ...

She put the scale up. We're running out of coffee. The scooper's in the dishwasher. I'll use one of the spoons. 6g. 15g. 25g. 16g. 25g. 18g. 23g. 19g. 22g. Leave it. Needs to be strong.

— You were saying about your date?
— He was cool.
— ...
— ...
— I'm going to need more than that.

Fucked up the bloom.

— He's a painter. Works out of this studio downtown. He showed me around.

— That's fun. What does he paint?

— Hella abstract stuff.

— Real.

Fucked up the first pour.

— But he seems . . .

— . . .

— I dunno. A little aloof.

— You don't like that?

— We can't both be.

— That's fair.

Fucked up the second pour.

— Are you going to see him again?

— Yeah, fuck it, why not?

She laughs and then looks at me.

— See now if you ever decided to go on a date, think of all the gossip we could have.

— . . .

— The whole house!

— . . .

Third pour exactly.

She looks back at him.

— She's grumpy this morning.

Almost drained.

— Our moody queen.

Drained.

He's staring at my ring.

Drafting in Bed

I know this will hurt.

Deciding Against It

Deleted.

Again

I know this will hurt.

Text From the Other Room

actually tho are you okay?

Text a Few Minutes Later

sorry if i was too mean !

Going Back to the Living Room and Sitting on the Worse Couch and Drinking Coffee

She turns as I come in but doesn't say anything to me; they keep talking.

Thirty Minutes Later

He leaves to go run an errand; she waits a bit.
— This isn't about the concert, is it?
— No.
— . . .
— . . .
— . . .
— I'm just . . . you know.
— I really don't.
— It's fine, really, it's been worse.
— . . .
What does she want me to say?
— . . .
Are you having an episode?
She fiddles with the curtain. She looks sad.
— And how are you doing?
— I'm good.
— That's good.
I smile at her; she doesn't believe it.
— You don't have to talk to me about it if you don't want
to.
— . . .
— Just as long as you're safe.
— I am.
— That's all I care about.
— I am.
— Good.
— . . .

— ...
— ...
— ...

Four Days Later

— Are you off this week?

She's here to make oatmeal.

— Using what's left of my time off, and then I'm going to quit.

— Really?

— Think it's time for something new.

— I guess that makes sense.

— ...

— I can look to see if there's anything open at my company.

For me?

— That'd be great, thanks.

She grabs the oatmeal, slides her right headphone back over her ear, and turns to face the stove.

What page was I on?

He walks in now.

— Hey.

— Hey.

He looks at her, but she's still facing the stove and hasn't seen, or heard, him.

— She's cooking.

— Yeah.

He sits on the worse couch.

— What's your day looking like?

— I'm off today, so probably just going to hang out, read a little maybe. You?

— Emails.

— . . .

— Always emails.

She's turned around.

— Oh, hey, didn't see you come in.

She smiles, and he watches her move from the stove and come to sit next to me.

— . . .   — . . .   — . . .

She pulls out her phone and scrolls a little.

— It is the hottest day ever in Vietnam.

— . . .   — . . .

— And they're putting in the new bike lane on Valencia.

— . . .   — . . .

— Those are the updates.

The oatmeal's making noises; she heads back to the stove.

— Did you change the jewel?

He's staring at the ring. Intently.

— It looks whiter.

— Just the light, I think.

— . . .

— . . .

— . . .

— Think I'm going to go for a walk.

Walk

He knows.

Home Again

The oatmeal's half-eaten on the counter; neither of them are home.

I grab my computer off the coffee table and head to my room.

Space Update

There's blood smeared across the top of his door.
Nobody answers. Nobody answers.
Nobody answers.

Back Home, Again

I'm sitting in bed when his texts come. First two pictures: one of her, one of the modeling guy, both tied up and gagged, both bleeding. Next an address. Then *Come*. Then *Bring the ring*. Then *Now*.

Excruciating Bus Ride

Everyone knows.

In the Apartment

The door is ajar, and when I open it, she's not there, neither of them are there, no one's there, nothing's there, just pages and pages and pages scattered across a blood-stained floor.

I pick one up. 12pt and double-spaced. *Loathe to have become what can only be described as deliriously high-*

I put it down. The blood is gone. The pages are gone. Even the one I just put down is gone.

I am alone in an empty apartment.

Outside, Again

It's sunnier, now: a woman with an endearingly violent wolf cut squats next to a small dog and speaks to it in stern but affectionate Portuguese; behind her, a pile of yet-to-be-scooped shit makes a modest claim on the noses of preoccupied passersby, who, predictably, are not really paying attention, concerned as they are with their busy, emotionally demanding lives; behind the dog shit, there's an assemblage of chairs and wooden planks that—were it not sitting in the middle of the street, roped off by yellow caution tape—could easily be mistaken for some sort of religious altar; there's another dog walker; there's a regular walker; there's a mobile phone call; there's me, now, passing the café:

— . . . to clarify, I would never use the expression *white genocide* . . .

— . . . no but like yes . . .

— . . . of course I think it looks good on you, everything . . .

— . . . what like some Series B shit? . . .

Up ahead, a woman steps into the crosswalk, anticipating that the light will turn green, which it doesn't, as there's a protected left turn, something the woman has just realized, stepping back onto the sidewalk, a little bashfully, even though she thinks no one has noticed.

Stoop Encounter

The steps to the apartment are covered in dirt, which suggests that my attempts at telepathic, interspecies diplomacy have failed and our erstwhile détente is now, well, erstwhile. Casualties of today's corvine assault include my thyme plant and a few of the lesser succulents—in exchange, the crow appears to have left a pair of carefully arranged french fries on the doorstep, solely, one has to imagine, to fuck with us.

I open the door.

— You're back early.

She's full lounge on the better couch.

I reflexively look down the hallway.

— He's still surfing, I think.

— …

— You okay?

— What?

— You look confused.

— …

— Perplexed, even.

— I'm good.

— If you say so.

She returns to her computer for a few seconds before:

— Oh!

— What's up?

— You got a weird letter.

— What's weird about it?

— Look on the table.

Inside of the brown envelope on the table, there is an unsigned note.

The Unsigned Note Inside of the Brown Envelope

Your eligibility for the FICTION trial has been confirmed. Please return with this letter in hand at your earliest convenience. We look forward to seeing you.

It Hits

I'm in her story.

And

That's how they got out.

Still in the Kitchen

I twist the ring.
Nothing changes.
— What's it say?
— Think it's just a crank.
— I wonder how they got our address.
— I don't know. There's no name. Maybe our neighbors got them too.
— Maybe.
I put the letter in my bag and head to my room, pausing, as I pass his room, to look inside it—it's the old stuff.
I twist the ring.
Nothing changes.
The jewel is almost entirely white.

Conclusion

Why me?

Eating Dinner

She finishes scraping the inside of her bowl.
— You've been kind of weird today.
— . . .
— More so than usual, I mean.
— My bad.
— You know, I think it's okay.
— . . .
— I appreciate your commitment to staying accountable.
— . . .
— Do you mind if I watch something?
— Go ahead.
— Yay.

The First Few Minutes of Season Two, Episode Two of *Find Your Voice* (2022–present)

As she's explained, she's still a few episodes out from the reveal, when the contestants will finally get to meet the romantic interests they've been talking to and building connections with, albeit, unseen, through a voice scrambler, which, in addition to the few but incredibly strict *Find Your Voice* conversational rules, has prevented them from determining their romantic interests' gender, a gambit that should, mid-season, make for some very stressful minutes of television.

The Second Few Minutes of Season Two, Episode Two of *Find Your Voice* (2022–present)

I'm really not in the mood.

Trying to Sleep

Maybe this is just life now.

Back at Work

She opens the door, and I can hear kids yelling in the other room.

— Hey, I'm from Solidarity Greens.

— Did y'all change names?

— Sorry?

— When I placed the order, I'm pretty sure it was like Comrades Deal or something like that.

— . . . right, yes, I got confused.

— . . .

— Well, anyways, here is this week's delivery. We've got a few good strains in there.

— Thanks.

— No problem, have a good one.

— You too.

Comrades Deal.

Sidewalk Sight

Three young women in day glo vests herd around one and a half dozen much younger children in day glo vests, who are all holding onto a rope and saying curious sentences as they dawdle along.

Ordering Lunch at the Sandwich Spot

— What can I get for you today?
— Can I get a Veggie Fiesta?
— Good choice.
— . . .
— Anything else?
— No, that's alright.
He flips the screen around, jauntily.

Eating Lunch in the Park

There's a wig party, and as you might imagine, the three men wearing judicial curls are debating somewhat furiously: the subject appears to be the domestication of horses in the Americas: the tallest one is wrong but winning—a woman in an explosive blue afro is looking for her keys; a man in red pigtails has an outfit to match; harsh bobs abound.

A quick vibe check of the park suggests that the people are having a good time and the canine experience is mixed.

It's sunny.

Sandwich is pretty good. Tapenade.

I should get back to work.

Work

As it always was.

Last Stop

It's her house. The door is slightly ajar, though I knock, though there's nothing, so I knock again, and there's still nothing, which almost certainly means she's dead, lying in her apartment, blood pooling on the floor, a hole in her head, still smelling like-

— Come in!

Everything looks the same: same green stools, same books, same busy counter—*it's lived in!*

She's sitting on the couch.

— Hey!

— Hey.

— ...

— ...

— What?

— Nothing.

She smiles.

— Were you expecting someone else?

— ...

She extends a hand and what smells like a spliff.

— It's the last of the Sloth.

I grab it; our fingers touch; she's still smiling; I inhale, and the world shatters.

Sitting in an Empty Living Room

The counter is clean. The sink is empty. He's not in his room. She's not in her room. I check my phone. One missed call and a text with the name of the restaurant. His family dinner. Fuck.

Looking for a Sweater

No. No. No. Yeah, sure.

Looking for Pants

Sure.

Wallet

Where it always is.

Keys

With the wallet.

Phone

bus is super delayed
i'll be there soon
sorry!!!

Waiting for the Bus

Come on.

On the Bus

I hear the sirens wail.

Nine, Ten, Eleven, Twelve, Thirteen, Fourteen, Fifteen, Sixteen, Seventeen, Eighteen, Nineteen, Twenty, Twenty-One, Twenty-Two, Twenty-Three, Twenty-Four, Twenty-Five, Twenty-Six, Twenty-Seven, Twenty-Eight, Twenty-Nine, Thirty, Thirty-One, Thirty-Two, Thirty-Three, Thirty-Four, Thirty-Five, Thirty-Six, Thirty-Seven

They keep wailing.

Hours Later

— Hello? . . . yeah, speaking . . . his emergency contact, he's alive? . . . oh thank fucking God . . . yes . . . yes . . . on Geary? . . . yes . . . I understand . . . when can I come?

A News Report in the Hospital Waiting Room, Playing Out of Someone's Phone

— A city-wide manhunt continues, as police search for those responsible for a San Francisco bombing that killed twenty-nine and injured dozens more yesterday evening. Witnesses-
A nurse is standing in front of me.

Hospital Room

He's in bed, unconscious; somehow, he manages to grimace when I walk into the room.

— …

— …

— …

— …

— …

— …

— …

— …

— …

— …

— You better not fucking die.

— …

— …

— …

He twitches and mouths what seems to be a word.
Then nothing. His face is empty.
He's breathing.
I watch him for a little longer, then I twist the ring.

Shabbat, Part III

I'm maybe six yards behind them, or us, I guess. I remember this summer. We're sitting on the top of the hill that overlooks the middle school; the city glints a few miles away. His hair is long, and mine is short. It smells like bad weed. It's warm. You can hear the owls and the crickets.

— What's it like there?

— It's alright.

— . . .

— Different.

— . . .

— I don't know.

— ` . . .

— It's hard to explain.

— I'll grade generously.

— It's . . . you know, I feel like being back here with y'all . . . it's just different.

— What do you mean?

— Everyone there just has this like . . . Vision, you know. He laughs.

— So do you.

— . . .

— And there are worse things to have.

— For sure.

— . . .

— I mean everyone's nice.

— I bet.

— I just . . .

— . . .

— It's just different.

— Could be worse.

— . . .

— For instance, you could be bringing them queso.

— Yeah.

— . . .

— Are you going to try and get a new job?

He smiles at the younger me.

— Doing what?

The younger me and the younger him smoke a moment in silence; he looks at me again.

— But you're happy there?

Why did I lie?

— Well shit that's all there is to it then.

— . . .

— You did good, man.

— . . .

The joint's out. They sit in silence. A car drives down the hill.

I twist the ring.

Broken

The room is darker—I look at the window, which is filled by a giant eye. It's mostly black, as are the feathers surrounding it. It looks from me to him to me to him to me to him and then to me again, then it takes off, its giant black wings wiping out the sun as it starts what sounds like a thousand car alarms.

Acknowledgments

Many thanks once again to Avery D'Agostino for their careful proofreading and to Zhanpei Fang for the beautiful cover art.

Thank you to the writers I shared early versions of this work with: Tom Cusano, Nate Brown, Thayer Anderson, Anna Sudderth, Oriana Tang, Maddie Kim, Molly Montgomery, Kion You, and Jordan Cutler-Tietjen.

Friends, family, Claudia—I owe you my life, and certainly this novel.